THE WITCH'S
CONSORT

(The First Witch Book 2)

Meg Xuemei X

Copyright © 2017 by Meg Xuemei X

First Edition
Silver Wheel Publishing

ISBN: 978-0-9979963-7-1

Printed in the United States of America

Cover art by Lou Harper
Edited by Monique Fischer

The Witch's Consort

My name is Freyja. I will soon cease to exist unless I acquire a cure from the Fey in the twilight realm. The Fey Empress will kill me if she learns that I'm an abomination—a Nephilim. And I'm not just the spawn of any Angel, but the monstrous Angel King she beheaded.

The smoking-hot, formidable Dragonian prince, my abductor, knows nothing about my curse, or that I am his fated mate— The First Witch—he is desperately searching for. As we draw close to the Fey territory, a horde of my father's former sentinels captures me. They plan to harvest my magic and drain me to resurrect the Dark Lord of All Angels—my evil grandfather.

The prince comes for me and saves me from the horrific fate, yet he still has to choose either the First Witch, or me as the wolf girl. Though his passion for me burns hotter than flame, a Dragonian never strays from a decided course. He believes if he picks me, he'll lose his future mate and the great kingdom she's meant to bring him. He doesn't know the witch and the wolf girl are one and the same. If he chooses the witch instead of me—hot, fresh, eager and right in front of him—he'll lose both.

TABLE OF CONTENTS

CHAPTER 1

The Hunters

My name is Freyja, the First Witch. The Dragonian prince Ares Darken and his six warriors know me as the wolf girl. Assisted by the Oracle, Ares located me in my forest home and forced me to leave my pack to find the First Witch for him.

Clueless that I was her, he was convinced the witch was his fated mate.

We'd been on the bumping road until I ditched him just now.

I gave him what he wanted—a witch, but a fake one.

I lied to him—naturally—and told him that the noblewoman in the store was his true mate. While they gazed upon each other as if they had both just discovered the wonders of the universe, I took off.

I broke the yoke the half-blood prince imposed on me, yet freedom didn't taste as sweet as I thought. I hadn't expected to be entangled with Ares, but since he was the only man, save for the powerful druid, who could sustain my death touch, I'd been addicted to his scorching caress.

If he'd given me what I wanted, I'd have stayed with him like a junkie to drugs. But he refused to sate me, vowing to stay true to the First Witch he had yet to meet. He lusted after me, but he coveted her more. I had nothing to offer him other than a few nights of pleasure, but she would bring him the greatest kingdom on Earth.

The Oracle had screwed him over big time. Look at me. How could I bring him an empire? I couldn't even bring him a meal, and I'd constantly demanded he feed me.

I'd vowed to never reveal my true identity to anyone in order to preserve myself, protect myself. My father's Angel sentinels had been hunting me from the moment I'd been born.

My mother had died to keep me alive. The whole village where I'd been born had perished because of me. I was a Nephilim, an abomination, the first and only hybrid of an advanced human and Angel. I also had Fey essence in me.

But now was no time to dwell on my past. Just as I was about to sprint toward my sour-tasting freedom and put the smoking-hot Dragonian prince behind me, the Angels caught up with me.

In an alley no one dared enter, three Angels closed in on me: one from the sky, two from each end of the alleyway. Their massive black wings heaved behind their shoulders, their long swords flashing white in their hands.

My heart pumped with raw fear.

I assessed my situation.

I had no weapon at my disposal. The damned Dragonians had taken all of my angelblade—the only weapon that could bleed the Angels.

Ares had done me great damage by kidnapping and exposing me. Now while my hunters were hell-bent on murdering me or planning something worse, the prince and his noblewoman were drinking in the horny sight of each other.

I would die today. I wouldn't even get a chance to tell him my blood was on his hands rather than on the Angel monsters'.

The only small comfort was that I wasn't completely defenseless.

I was a weapon.

I prayed that the Angels hadn't learned about my lethal touch.

As soon as the eye-patched Angel swooped toward me with a serpentine smile on his cruel lips, I recognized my handiwork. I'd sunk an angelblade into his left eye at the bottom of the lake ten years ago.

Time sure had flown by.

I'd thought he was dead.

Swiftly, I stripped myself bare, my clothing piling at my feet. On top of the heap were the velvet gloves Merlin made for me.

No one could save me—not the great druid, not Fey, and definitely not the insufferable Dragonian prince.

I could only count on myself now.

Every inch of my bare skin was death. If humans touched me, they would die in agony in two seconds. It took three seconds for a Dragonian. Angels would last for seven long seconds.

My hunters gaped at my nakedness. When I spotted lust in the beautiful monsters' eyes, I felt hopeful and repulsed.

Come and touch, boys, I beckoned them, swaying my hips. *Let's play.*

But the Angels on the ground halted several yards from me. My heart stopped cold. Did they know about the lethalness of my skin?

My panic dissipated when I saw their heated gazes roving

over my breasts.

I brushed a nipple to spice things up and get their blood flow to their groins. I would need to be provocative. Violence and sex went hand in hand with their species.

"Hello again, *Princess*," the one with the eye-patch called, his good eye a burning dark coal.

I flashed him a syrupy smile and purred, "Hello, gorgeous. I've missed you. You look exotic with that patch. Is it homemade?"

"Freyja, right?" he asked. "You're all grown up."

His unforgiving smile sent chills down my spine. He'd learned my name. He'd followed me here. He'd watched Ares and me fuck. Why had he waited until now?

"How did you know I'm in Amathus?" I asked in a sweet voice.

Though I'd accumulated angelic data when I'd killed an Archangel and learned more about the alien predators' origin, I still had no idea how they knew about my existence in the first place. They hadn't been able to find me after I'd escaped them last time. I speculated that somehow my pack could shield me from their sight or maybe my forest blocked their probe. That protection must have expired when Ares dragged me out of my haven. He'd exposed me long enough for my enemies to track me down.

Eye-patch cocked his head. "Take a guess, *Princess*."

I really hated him for calling me that.

"Did you see me from a crystal ball?" I fished. Of course not. But I'd heard that they stored information in crystal devices. They had to have some kind of gadget to track me.

"I'll be happy to show you," Eye-patch said. "If you go with us nicely instead of kicking, screaming, and stabbing at me like last time."

It was good that he hadn't mentioned touching, which meant I had a fighting chance.

I pressed my back against the cold stone wall, so I could watch the three of them at the same time. I bent a knee, keeping my pose provocatively erotic.

"I've been waiting for you for a long time," I said. "Why show up now?"

As I tried to get them to talk, I noticed they were in no hurry to approach me. The Angels studied me with mixed menacing interest and lust. Their black wings remained arched and their hands gripped their swords.

I was a half Angel. While earthling weapons couldn't harm me, the angelblade would give me a fatal wound.

"Where did you hide, Princess, before you tangled up with the barbarians? Your grandfather will be disappointed in your dallying with the inferior races."

My heart skipped a beat. It was the first time he'd hinted who was behind this hunt—my evil grandfather. The former Dark Lord of All Angels had been the mightiest being in the universe before his heir, High Prince Seth, had shattered his essence.

But the Dark Lord didn't die. Rumor was he was hiding in the deepest void, seeking to return. It'd been decades, and Prince Seth's hunting party hadn't succeeded in flushing him out.

I laughed deceptively. "Then my grandfather should come to discipline me in person."

It was anyone's worst nightmare to be on the Dark Lord's hit list. He had no remorse and no restriction, even when it came to killing his own flesh and blood. He'd once let my father sever his heir's wings because the High Prince defied his order to harvest the Fey Empress' magic.

"The High Lord will do more than disciplining," Eye-patch chuckled, "after we take you to him."

My breath caught in my throat. My instinct had been right. My grandfather was a notorious power absorber. For eons, he'd gone around the galaxies to harvest great powers before his heir had blasted him off to defend his mate.

Now he wanted mine.

He must have known I was his son's spawn. He must have

sensed the darkness in me and thought it would boost him more than any other power, since we were of the same bloodline.

I tilted my head to regard Eye-patch. "I'd love to visit him, but isn't he too far away? I don't have a long life. He should hurry up and come to Earth, if he really wants to see his only granddaughter."

"The ship is waiting on the other side of the portal," Eye-patch said. "We can travel in light years. I'm sure you're also an immortal, like your father. Like us."

Eye-patch dropped the distance between us. He looked down at me from less than twenty feet in the air.

If I leaped and attacked him by surprise, I could at least grab his foot. I would climb up, touch his hand or his wing, and send him to an agonizing death. Then I would jump over the walls and roofs, land on the other side of the market place, and merge into the crowd.

To guarantee a success, I needed him to be closer and less guarded.

"Since my grandfather sent you to pick me up, shouldn't you kneel in front of your Princess? Where are your manners?"

The other two Angels blinked, but kept watching me like hawks on their sole prey.

Eye-patch barked a hateful laugh. "Under different circumstances, we would have to, Princess."

My biological father was no longer a king. He'd been burned by the Fey Empress and then beheaded by his own brother in their final battle.

"King Agro perished, but my grandfather still rules the universe," I said. That was a joke. The Dark Lord had been hunted. But these goons liked to think their master was still in charge. "He won't be pleased when he learns how his only granddaughter is treated."

"You grandfather won't care how we ship you," Eye-patch said. "As long as you're delivered and not completely dead."

A chill ran up my spine.

"Tell me how you killed two of my former associates, Princess," Eye-patch's voice turned icier and crueler, "and I'll make the whole process less gruesome for you."

My heart leapt with a small hope. He didn't know about my death touch.

"I can show you," I said with a sweeter smile, "with a hot kiss. You know I have a thing for Angels."

He stared at my mouth warily. "So you have His High Lord's power?"

What power exactly?

King Agro had been a dud—the shame had driven him to be the worst sadist and made him hate his half-brother, the High Prince, to the bone marrow. If he were alive, knowing the ancient, angelic royal power had skipped a generation but had chosen me, his bastard half-breed, I wondered if he would shriek and scream unceasingly.

Only, I didn't want this poisonous Angel power that had cursed me.

"I have Earth power from Goddess Rhea," I bluffed. "Empress Rose used the power to drive your kind out, and I'll do exactly the same. If your High Prince learns you're still here, he'll dwell upon you like an eagle on pigs. He isn't known to be merciful. So be gone. Now."

"You're shrewd, Princess," Eye-patch said. "But the High Prince has his hands full with his twins at the moment. His half-bred brats give him more trouble than the whole Fey nation."

"Then he'll want the streets to be clean of any vermin," I said. "I should give him a call. An Earth citizen should always do her duty."

"I doubt he'll be nicer to you than to me if he knows who you are," said Eye-patch.

"The princess might have the pulse power," chimed in a platinum-haired Angel, who guarded the north end of the alley.

"What pulse power?" Eye-patch asked, his eye staying on me.

"If you touch her, she pulses and kills," the platinum-haired Angel said. "His High Lord has it and can kill at will. Perhaps that's how she killed Ullrik and Zeno."

"We shall not touch her bare skin," the other Angel added his unworthy opinion. "She removed all of her clothing in order to murder us in cold blood."

"Activate your armor and grab her," Eye-patch ordered.

I bent my knees and doubled over, pretending to laugh at their ridiculous theory, only to leap toward Eye-patch like a flash before he could finish his sentence. I didn't inherit wings from my Angel side, but I could jump higher than any earthling.

I could have leapt onto the guardian's back easily each time, but I'd held back, not wanting Ares to learn about my strengths or weaknesses.

Eye-patch saw me coming and surged up.

I grabbed his left foot, though I had aimed for his neck. My other hand dragged down his trousers. If I could get an inch of his bare skin, I would make sure he stayed dead this time. As his trousers came down, his foot booted my head with a savage force. If I were a complete human, that kick would have broken my skull.

No mortals could sustain an Angel's strike.

My head didn't crack, but pain exploded inside.

I loosened my grip on Eye-patch.

As I fell, I spun in the air and threw myself at the closest Angel below. He hadn't expected my move. I always had tricks in my arsenal. I landed on his wings, grabbed his platinum hair, and shoved my hand to his neck.

He went down with a scream, his sword flying from him. The other Angel in the alley charged toward me, his blade thrusting at me while I still perched on his pal's back.

I twisted my torso and watched helplessly as the cold blade came not toward my heart but my shoulder. He planned to incapacitate me and then capture me. I couldn't avoid that thrust, but I would have the narrow window to slash my own throat before the angelblade went through me.

Whatever hideous plan my evil grandfather had for me, he could kiss its ugly butt goodbye. My corpse wouldn't do him any good. Let him hole up in his dark lair for eternity.

I drew out an angelblade strapped on my victim's thigh while he shrieked in agony. He had to suffer my burn for a few more seconds.

The Angel's blade punctured my skin. Just as I propelled my body forward toward its hilt to reach my enemy's hand

and give it a fine, final death touch, an enraged roar thundered beside me, "You won't touch her!"

A white flash slammed up against the Angel's sword that pricked beneath my shoulder blade. I pulled backwards at once, away from the crossing blades, and jumped up with the angelblade in my hand.

I thought I would never see Prince Darken again in my life, and there he was—attacking the Angel like a mad dog. The kind of brutality he exuded wasn't suited for a faint-hearted.

What was he doing here? Why wasn't he with his precious *witch*? I'd left him gawking at the noblewoman. She'd gazed up at him with white-hot desire and laid her elegant hand on his muscled arm to claim him.

I'd believed they'd go fuck each other's brains out after that, and my heart had bled at the mere thought.

But he was here, defending me.

Though my heart leapt with joy at the sight of him, I wondered why he'd left his *witch* so soon. He'd finally gotten what he'd wanted—the First Witch. She was a fake, but he wasn't aware of it. How could he have the strength to leave her behind and come for me?

His lips curled away from his teeth, which lengthened to fangs. Earth! I widened my eyes as he grew a foot taller. His physique broadened. His features changed to something more akin to a ferocious beast than that of a man.

I didn't allow myself to be mesmerized by his transformation. I needed to focus on taking down Eye-patch and keep Ares from getting killed.

That had been taken care of when thunderous roars announced the arrival of the guardians.

Ventus and Ignis tore into Eye-patch from the opposite direction, their jaws wide open and their iron fangs sharpened.

Their rapid movements blurred into one giant form as they fought.

However, the blur evened out when battle-hardened Eye-patch showed his deviousness. He shot out between the guardians and they crashed into each other. Ignis roared in pain and shot a mouthful of fire toward his foe, but Eye-patch's armor absorbed it.

Blood spattered on my face from the sky, and it wasn't the Angel's.

"Take me up!" I shouted. I could stand on a guardian's back and aide them.

Massive wings flapped rapidly toward us. Glacies and Mettalum bellowed their battle cries as they charged at Eye-patch.

Eye-patch tossed an angelblade at Glacies' head. Glacies reared down and the blade narrowly missed his neck, plunging into his shoulder instead. Glacies growled in fury, turned, and slammed into Eye-patch.

I had to leave the four guardians to bring him down. I needed to aid Ares with his fight against the Angel on the ground.

Ares' blade drew blood from the Angel, but his opponent sliced his leg. If I could get behind the Angel's back, we could sandwich him.

I could leap and land behind him, but it would end badly for me if he suddenly flew up and snatched me. I was willing to take the risk, though. I hated seeing Ares injured and bleeding.

I ran a few yards backwards. Before I could launch into a leap, Einarr emerged from the other end of the alley and lunged at the attacking Angel.

The Angel wheeled, hacking left and right to fend off Ares and Einarr. While the two warriors were thrown off by his sudden burst of force, the Angel shot up to the sky.

Mettalum emerged right above him, opened his massive mouth, and closed on the Angel's neck. The Angel thrashed about in Mettalum's jaw, trying to break from his grip as he brought his sword up to hack at the beast.

Earthling weapons couldn't harm an Angel. An earthling creature couldn't end the superior alien with a bite either. Ares leapt up, raised his angelblade, and sank it into the Angel's heart.

The Angel went limp and dropped his sword.

Eye-patch sent me a vengeful smile before he sped upward and fled, faster than a streak of lightning. Three of the guardians gave a chase. In a blink they were gone.

"I've flushed you out, *Princess*," Eye-patch's sinister voice reached me from distant somewhere. "We've got your blood imprint. The High Lord's army will come for you. We'll never cease hunting you until he has you. When I return, I'll gut your Dragonian hybrid in front of you. That's my promise to you for taking my eye out, Princess."

I couldn't help but trembled at the threat.

CHAPTER 2

Dark Lord

I'd obtained the horrific truth after touching the platinum-haired Angel, who had a direct link to his master. I wondered if Atlas—the Dark Lord of All Angels—had felt his vessel's agonizing death through the connection.

Atlas' legion had one urgent mission: hunt me down and ship me to him, so he could harvest my power to resurrect himself.

In the Angel war two decades ago, even after the High Prince's Sky Power and his Fey mate's Earth Magic had shattered Atlas' essence and ripped his immense power off him, the ex-ruler of the universe had survived, though not in one piece. A fragment of his power had wandered above Earth's atmosphere and found the Dark Lord's new bloodline. That power had targeted me, embedding itself into the fetus growing in my mother's belly before Atlas had vanished.

And now he wanted it back. He wanted the entity of darkness I'd caged at the bottom of an ice lake deep within me. Though it was locked away, it had become part of me.

If Atlas took it back, I would die.

He wouldn't give a damn about that. His army was more than desperate to help restore him. They wanted to reclaim the universe. They wanted to be the conquerors every species feared and worshipped. Their High Prince, who was now the most powerful Angel, didn't have the ambition to rule the cosmos. All he wanted was to be with his Fey mate in her Twilight Realm on Earth.

I was supposed to be the first lamb on the altar; my blood and magic would return my grandfather to his lost glory.

He discreetly dispatched his scouts to hunt me down, for fear of alarming the High Prince. But now that he'd seen me through the link, he wouldn't hesitate to send a legion after me.

They would come through the portal, endless streams of them. How soon would the first fleet reach Earth?

If High Prince Seth learned about this, he'd come out of the Twilight Realm to kill me before his father could harvest my dark soul to fuel his power. It was better to die at my uncle's hands than be drained by my grandfather.

I would strike a deal with the High Prince before I went down. His mate owed my mother a life debt, and I knew she would pay it back.

Hadn't I said if I had to go down, I would go down in style?

I could leave behind a legacy as the girl who prevented the ultimate evil from returning—not that I cared much about my legacy, but this planet also belonged to my pack.

So I'd stick to my decision to go to Mysth, where I had a better chance to fend off Atlas. I needed to hurry before the legion managed to get to me first.

I'd seen the Dark Lord as he'd seen me. If he became complete and gathered all of his essence, he would be as powerful as before, if not more. He would blanket the universe with his foul darkness.

Cold washed over me, and it wasn't because I was naked.

My teeth clattered violently as I went to fetch my clothing.

Ares reached me while I trembled so hard I couldn't get a foot into my panties. He went down on one knee, placed me on his lap, and helped me pull up my undergarment.

Lucas leapt from Ignis and landed near me. Rage and worry distorted his boyishly handsome face. He rushed toward me. Ares could touch me, but the shifter would end up dead.

Lucas fetched my cloak.

"Don't touch me!" I cried, a bit harsher than I intended.

He froze, hurt flashing through his warm, brown eyes.

"I won't touch you," he said. "I'll only cover you."

Ares cut Lucas a glare and yanked my cloak from his hand.

"My skin is bad for you," I told the shifter in a shivering voice, but he didn't buy it as he looked at me then at Ares.

"The prince will have to wash the toxins off his hands," I said. "I don't want you or anyone else to be contaminated."

"I wouldn't mind," Lucas said softly.

"I don't want to harm you," I said.

"Return to Ignis and stay on guard, Lucas," Ares ordered in a hard tone as he moved my hand into my cloak's sleeves and tied it around me. "The Angels might return with greater numbers."

Looking dejected, Lucas mounted Ignis.

As soon as I was fully dressed, Ares rose, pulled me up, and crashed me against his chest so tightly I could barely breathe. Somehow, his solid warmth and scent solaced me. I grabbed the front of his coat and clung to him, afraid darkness would suck me into its hole and transport me to the most evil being if I let go of the Dragonian warrior.

Ares had been in the grip of rage, but now he trembled in fear. "I almost lost you, Freyja," he said in a ragged breath. I'd never seen him so vulnerable.

If he'd been two seconds late, the Angels would have gotten me. They'd have carried my corpse to Atlas.

I sniffed against his shoulder, grateful at my narrow escape. "Thank you."

"I won't let them have you," he said fiercely, his hand in my tangled flaming hair, trying to smoothen it. "I won't let them near you again. I won't let anyone harm you."

He'd heard Eye-patch's threat.

My immortal enemies would hunt me to the end of the universe, and no mortal army on Earth could fight off the Angel horde.

But Ares' vow stopped me from shivering.

"The horde will come for me," I said.

"I'll cut all of them down!" Ares snarled.

"You're better off leaving me here," I said. "I won't blame you."

"Never," he said. "Never leave you."

"What about your witch?" I asked, suddenly remembering the noblewoman. "Where is she?"

Ares gave me a withering look, despite that a moment ago

he'd been fiercely protective and almost tender toward me.

"Look at this Angel, Ares," Einarr called from a few yards away.

Oh, crap!

In my distraught, I'd totally forgotten about the Angel that I'd burned to death. I should have turned him around and laid him face down before I'd left his corpse. It was too late now to cover the Angel's gray, cracked skin.

Ares turned his head and fixed his eyes on the Angel's body. Two trails of smoke wafted from the Angel's blackened eye. It was creepy.

I untangled myself from Ares' hold and followed him to the Angel's side, staring down at the corpse and trying to think of a good explanation for the phenomenon.

"He died just like—" Ares stopped and looked at me, his puzzled expression turning grim, then unreadable.

He'd seen the same features on the Dragonian and the human raiders whom I'd killed in the forest on our first day together. He hadn't registered how strange it was that I'd perched atop an Angel, completely naked and clutching the alien's face in my hands when he'd rushed to my rescue. He hadn't cared about the Angel's screams of agony until now.

The prince's eyes drifted to my gloved hands.

He was piecing everything together. And this time, I

couldn't credit the kill to Goddess Rhea.

"Freyja," he started.

I stared back at him blankly, holding an angelblade.

Before I could back myself to the stone wall, Ventus, Glacies, and Mettalum returned with roars, wind, and flapping wings.

"We lost the Angel," Ventus cursed.

"Let's move out before he brings more of his kind," Ares ordered.

Strangely, no one in the market place seemed to realize there had been a raging battle around. It was as if the alley was a dead zone.

CHAPTER 3

The Prince

We left the city of Amathus and headed south.

I sat in front of Ares on Ventus' back. We were both silent, but Ares hadn't removed his arm from around my waist. I slouched against him, the side of my face pressing on his sculpted chest.

I needed the haven of his warmth, though I dreaded the questions he was going to ask.

The guardians were still thrilled from battling with the Angels. Ares and his team couldn't hear their telepathic chats, but I heard everything loud and clear.

The Angel was strong and fast, Ventus said.

When he comes back, Glacies snarled, *his ass is mine.*

Any wound from an angelblade was hard to heal and I was sure Glacies' shoulder was searing with pain. If he were an ordinary beast, he'd be dead by now.

They marked the witchling, Ignis said.

We'll defend her, Mettalum said.

I'd thought he wasn't happy with me after I'd called him Metty.

That Angel wore an eye-patch because of our witchling, Ignis said. *She stabbed him. Wake her up, Ventus. I want to know the details.*

Freyja? Ventus called in my head.

I ignored him. I wasn't in a high spirit as he was. Plus, I didn't want Ares' attention on me.

"Freyja, wake up!" Ventus shouted. "I have a question."

Ares growled. "Leave her alone, Ventus. She needs rest. When we get to a safer location, Einarr will take care of her and check on you all again."

The tip of the angelblade had pierced my skin under my shoulder blade. Einarr had tried to tend to me, but I'd refused to let him touch me. I'd also refused to let Ares inject the serum into me.

"We need to treat your injury," Ares had said. "The wound from an angelblade is the worst case."

"It's only a graze," I had said.

"Even a graze from their blade will cause a serious infection on a mortal."

"The serum won't work on me. It'll mess me up."

"How do you know?"

"I learned that when I was a child," I'd said. "Any drug will do me more harm than good." At his worried expression, I'd added, "It'll heal on its own."

He had simply cleaned me and bandaged me. "We'll need to monitor you. If you run a fever—"

"There will be no fever," I'd cut him off. "And I don't need a nursemaid."

He hadn't insisted on getting his way. Though from his dark look, I knew he had simmering questions for me. He hadn't pushed, but had put me in front of him on Ventus. His arm hadn't left my waist ever since.

After a couple of hours of quiet flying, my body relaxed a fraction.

Ares definitely noticed I was less clingy.

I could feel the questions burning on the tip of his tongue, and I had a few of my own burning hot. Most of them concerned the lovely noblewoman.

"Feeling better?" he asked.

"Uh," I said vaguely.

"Are you scared of me?" he asked.

I gave him a sidelong glance. "Why must I be afraid of you?"

"You saw my beast form. No other women have ever seen it."

"I've seen worse monsters, Ares."

He didn't seem happy with the answer. "You compare me to those monsters?"

"You want me to be scared? Fine. I'm still shivering from the sight of your enhanced form. Please don't eat me. I beg you, Your Highness. I'm all bones."

He shook his head. "Other than your own comfort and freedom and your pack, you don't take anything seriously, do you?"

I took my hunters very seriously, but I didn't tell him that.

"But at least your annoying traits are back," he said, "which means you're now normal."

"Is it normal for me to say thank you?"

He sighed and tucked me closer to him. "Why do you keep running away from me, Freyja?" he asked in a composed voice, but I heard exhaustion, hurt, and repressed anger in it. "You almost got yourself killed."

"Yes, enlighten us, why did you run away from us, Freyja?" Ventus echoed. "We've been good to you. Do you even care that I was frightened when Ares told me you were missing? Who else could protect you better than us? I'm disappointed in you. Very disappointed."

Now he was disenchanted. When he'd driven Eye-patch away and come back for me, he'd brushed my side with his snout to comfort me. It had made my throat tight. I hadn't wanted to form any bond with anyone outside of my pack, but I'd started cherishing his friendship more than I knew.

"I'll forgive you if you tell me how you maimed the Angel and took out his eye," Ventus continued. "When was that? I wanted every juicy detail."

"Ventus," Ares snapped. "I'm doing the questioning here."

"I was helping," the guardian of wind said.

"You aren't helping," Ares said. "You're distracting."

"Never mind me," Ventus said, his left shoulder rising and falling in a half shrug. Next, he might roll his eyes to the back and could see how tightly Ares held me.

"Freyja," Ares said, "I told you over and over you need to learn—"

"Where is your witch?" I asked.

"Don't know and don't care," he said.

"Did you let her go?" I asked incredulously.

He snarled. I knew his niceness wouldn't last.

"How could you let her get away?" I said indignantly. "I secured her for you!"

What witch? Ventus asked in my head.

"Secured her for me?" Ares sneered. "You tried to tie me down to a fake witch!"

I blinked. How had he figured that out? Now he was going to get really mad if I didn't find a way to appease him.

"Did you ask her if she was the First Witch?" I asked.

"I didn't need to ask," he said, almost smugly.

"You won't know if she or anyone is the witch or not," I argued. "Only I can validate it for you."

"Don't be so sure, wolf girl. You aren't the only one who's got pure instinct. I would know it if she were the witch."

Then this big idiot should know I was the witch, but he had no idea. No idea at all.

I gibed at him. "Enlighten me?"

"I didn't feel anything for that woman."

"It's not for you to feel, Ares. It's for you to trust and accept my judgment."

"Who do you think I am?" he asked. "You think I'll let you trick me so easily? You think I'll accept a fraud?" But he contained his fury, considering the ordeal I'd just gone through.

I frowned at him. "I didn't expect you to be picky."

He scoffed. "When I meet my witch, I'll be on fire," he said, then glanced down at me. I kept my expression demure, and his look turned forlorn on top of his predatory hunger for me. "Maybe it won't be like the kind of fire I have with you, but I should at least feel something, something strong."

My heart leapt. He'd just unwittingly admitted his feelings for me.

"But you did feel strongly for Agatha," I said. "Is her name Agatha? You just aren't good at admitting your feelings."

"If she were my witch and I had feelings for her, she'd be in my arms right now."

And here I was—in his arms.

Ventus was particularly quiet as he focused on eavesdropping on our conversation.

Shouldn't you pay attention to flying, Ventus? I reminded him.

"I knew you lied to me the moment I let go of your shoulders outside the dressing room," Ares said.

"If you'd known I was lying, you wouldn't have stared at her as if she was the wonder of the wonders," I said, unable to let go of the last image I'd seen before I'd left them to their devices.

He narrowed his amber eyes on me. "When did I do that?"

"I saw you two drink in the horny sight of each other before I left the store. You were into her, even though she wasn't your witch. You're just so good at lying to yourself. Anyway, I don't even care. I'm only shocked that you lost her."

"You do care, and you're still jealous."

"If I were jealous, Ares Darken, I'd have taken her down the moment she laid her claws on you." I'd almost done just that. "But I let you have her, didn't I? I even encouraged you."

His dark anger returned, his voice promising a punishment after my recovery. "So you admit you intentionally misled me?"

"I was trying to help," I said innocently.

"You've tried to screw me over at every turn ever since I took you in!"

"That's not true. You tend to think the worst of me."

"Tell me one good thing you've ever done."

"I told you about your half-brother wanting you dead," I said, putting down a finger for my first good deed. "You haven't thanked me for the priceless information, and I didn't even charge you a penny for the valuable intel." I put down a second finger. "Third, I prevented you from foolishly nose-diving into the safe house to be toasted by an army of skilled bounty hunters." Four fingers went down. "I've been cooperating with the guardians. I led you to the rabbit stews in Merlin's house. I provided entertainment for you on the road. And before I came with you, I ordered my wolves not to tear your throat out. That wasn't easy."

He stared at me incredulously.

"The list can go on, but I only have ten fingers and ten toes," I said. "Even now I'm still doing a good deed, leading you south toward your coveted witch. And Your Highness, instead, exposed me and led me to danger. How fair is it?"

"Twisted lies," he said. "When you lie, you carry this calm air to try to convince people. Your face becomes blank and you make firm eye contact."

I made a mental note to correct my tell the next time I lied. Now I needed to further distract him from asking me the questions I dreaded.

"So what happened to your pretty, refined, and sophisticated noble lady?" I asked.

When Ares had had his first hard-on for me, he'd been displeased. He'd told me straight in my face, *"You aren't even my type. I prefer refined, sophisticated females."*

The prince gave me a sour look, his thumb and finger holding my chin. "Will you turn everything I said against me?"

Even that challenging touch brought me electrifying pleasure. I held my breath and arched an eyebrow, signaling I was waiting for an answer.

"I didn't stay with Agatha long," he said. "When I returned to the second floor and you were gone, I lost my mind." He swallowed. "I panicked. All I wanted was to find you. Nothing else mattered."

His vulnerability made something flutter in my chest.

"Not even the witch?" I asked.

He snarled. "She isn't the witch. We've established that."

I sighed at his temper.

"I forgot about her and everything," he said. "I didn't even bother to say a word to her when I ran out of the shop to track you. I remembered Merlin said you were being hunted and I had the worst feeling. I summoned Einarr and the guardians. When I found you in that damned alley and saw that fucker swinging his sword at you—" He stopped, unable to continue. But a second later, he was the hard Dragonian prince again. "Don't you ever do that to me again, Freyja. Stop running! You'll have your freedom when the time comes, but not sooner, and not at the risk of your life. I'll make a good arrangement for you and you'll have a comfortable, safe life when this is over. While we're searching the true witch, I'll protect you."

He still coveted his witch more than anyone and anything. So, it was true that a Dragonian never strayed from a set path, and Prince Darken would never abandon his ambition.

His lust for me was just lust. It was nothing compared to what he thought the First Witch would offer him. He would continue to risk me for her. The warmth I had felt when he'd told me how he had come for me vanished.

My face grew cold, and it wasn't because of the icy current.

"I've never been as afraid as I was when I saw the Angels—" Ares said.

"Angels are fearsome species," I said flatly, interrupting him.

"I do not fear them," he said, his voice cold with rage. "I was nearly paralyzed today because I thought I'd been too late. I thought I lost you."

"If I perish," I said, "you should return to the Oracle and ask for a refund."

His arm tightened around me. "Don't say that," he said gruffly. "You won't be harmed under my watch. But I'll have to think of something to prevent you from running away again."

"If you think you can chain me," I said, my voice harder than ice, "you'll be making the biggest mistake in your life."

"I'll never chain you," he said, "but I can't allow you to be so ruthless and put yourself in danger."

I let cold silence stretch between us.

He shook his head. "Why are we quarreling? I just got you back." He tugged me against his hard chest and buried his face on my hair. "I just got you back," he murmured, inhaling my scent.

I started crying.

I shouldn't cry. I'd survived the Angel attack. I had Ares back, even if it was temporary. The Angel's threat was terrifying, but that wouldn't make me sob.

I blamed it on Ares' chest being so warm and cozy.

"Hush," he said, squeezing me, his large hand patting my head.

That only made me sniff harder.

"Hey," he said, "I'm here. I won't let anything bad happen to you."

Until he found his witch.

He scooped me onto his lap and pulled my face a few inches away from his chest so he could wipe my tears away with his thumb, but they just kept streaming down, faster than he could dry them.

He rocked me in his arms and murmured unintelligible words that sounded like a lullaby. He'd never been so tender with me, and so I quickly found something I could complain about.

"You were respectful and gentle to the noblewoman," I said, my voice breaking. "You've never been sweet with me. You always yell at me."

"Not always," he said. "I can be tender and caring to you, but you drive me mad most of the time, and the rest of the time I can't think straight around you, especially when you—" he sighed, then chuckled. "All of this sniveling is because I was nice to another female? I don't get you, Freyja. I didn't even flirt with her. But if you're sour about it, you have only yourself to blame. You set me up with her. Speaking of which, there'll be consequences . . ."

I didn't hear the rest of his threats or comforts as I fell asleep on his solid, warm chest with hot tears on my face.

CHAPTER 4

The Mountains

The guardians alighted under a ridge of snowy mountains. They could go no further since Ignis and Glacies were injured. Their wounds hadn't sealed. The serum Einarr carried didn't really help genetically-enhanced beasts that much. Like me, they had to recover through the natural healing process. So Ares decided we would stay in the mountains for a few nights until the guardians regained their strength.

The Dragonians set up the tents. I didn't like any of them, but they were efficient when it came to things like that.

To my delight, a camp fire was lit in no time. Jericko, the Dragonian with the bluest skin, was boiling water. I would remind them to go hunting if they hadn't moved in the next hour.

I didn't like to go hungry before bedtime.

While I took in the surroundings with my hands on my hips, surveying everything, Ares strode toward me. My pulse spiked. Electric currents charged the air. It happened whenever he entered my proximity for the first time, and my body always reacted with giddy lust.

"Freyja," he ordered, "I need to treat your wound. Sit on the rock over there."

"It's only a scrape," I said, not intending to move.

"Even if it's a scratch, the surrounding area might have been infected. Any wound—even tiny—from an angelblade isn't a light matter. We have to cut out the bad flesh. There's no other way around. Einarr will give you a pain killer. It'll be a minor surgery, and I'll hold your hand the whole time. It'll be fast."

"I don't need surgery," I said.

"Freyja!" Ares raised his voice. "This isn't time for stubbornness. The infection could kill you! Must I hold you down?"

The Dragonians stopped their tasks and looked in our direction. The guardians snapped their heads and peered at me. Ignis and Glacies hunched close to the mountains, and Ventus guarded their brethren. Mettalum had gone on patrol with Lucas.

Einarr gathered the medic kits.

I sighed. Ares wouldn't let it go unless he saw it. I tore the bandage from my supposed wound.

"Freyja, let Einarr handle it," Ares said.

The small cut from the angelblade had closed up. There wasn't even a scar on my skin, except for a trace of dried blood below my shoulder blade.

"See, I'm as good as new," I said.

Ares leaned closer to check my skin.

Einarr was at our side the next second, his eyes widening. "No mortal can heal from a wound inflicted by an angelblade," he said, handing Ares a medical wipe, and the prince cleaned the dried blood from my shoulder.

"Don't look at me like I'm not an earthling mortal," I said, going on the offense. "Do you need to see my birth certificate?" As if I had one.

"This is impossible," Ares said.

"Nothing is impossible, Prince," I said. "Before your time, no one believed a hybrid like you was a possible."

"How did you heal?" Ares asked.

"Shouldn't you be happy I can regenerate quickly, like you?" I said. "Less trouble for you on the road."

I wouldn't volunteer the information that only an angelblade could bleed me.

"Of course, I'm happy you're recovered," Ares said, looking at the dirty wipe and tossing it away. "We'll get your blood sample when we get to Atlantis."

Over my dead body.

Ares must have seen something savage flash through my eyes, because he tensed immediate.

"What is it, Freyja?" he demanded.

Treat me like a lab animal and you'll regret your life. I vow it on my mother's grave.

"Merlin gave me this ability to heal myself," I lied, then remembered what Ares had said about my tell. So, instead of looking straight at him, I dropped my gaze, hoping I looked demure. "That was his parting gift to me."

Ares just studied me, as did Einarr.

I controlled the urge to draw a circle with the tip of my foot, which would for sure tell them how nervous I was. I counted to four before I brought my gaze back to Ares' face.

He didn't seem convinced at all, but he didn't discredit me either. Maybe he took pity on me and decided to cut me some slack. I'd been weeping in his arms an hour ago. Perhaps he was out of sorts from my tears? If that was the case, I should cry more often.

"The druid said you were being hunted," Ares said, his voice filled with purpose, "but I didn't expect them to be

Angels. Why do they hunt you?"

"Fuck if I know. They're psychotic," I said, my eyes brightening in a mock realization. "Perhaps it's the same reason you hunted me? They must want me to lead them to the First Witch."

"Like hell I'll let them near my witch," Ares growled.

My words worked to distract him, yet his truth hammered into my heart—his witch was far more important than I was.

"I don't think anyone knows about her existence, except for the druid, the Oracle, and us," Einarr said.

"Angels are resourceful," I said. "If we know about her, then they have to know. She has great power since she's the First Witch. Perhaps a high-ranking Archangel wants her as his mate, as King Agro once took the Fey Empress to be his bride."

Ares narrowed his eyes, his face hardening as he stared at me. He hadn't met the mysterious witch, but he was already so protective and possessive of her. A sudden resentment and jealousy toward both the prince and the witch expanded in me.

"You said you killed an Archangel before?" Ares drawled. "Is that the Angel with the patch on his left eye?"

The interrogation had started. I'd have to let him get it over with. Sooner or later, he would chase me with all the questions, and best to do it now.

"I didn't expect him to survive," I said. "I should have thrown the dagger harder. I should have ensured he was dead."

"You threw a dagger at me the moment you saw me, without taking a second to ask me a question," Ares said in disapproval.

"I thought we'd decided to put that behind us," I said.

He nodded. "I was fast enough to block it. The Angel we fought today is just as fast as I am. I wonder how you managed to land your dagger in his eye."

The Dragonian prince was sly. He had set up a trap for me before I knew.

"He was busy molesting me," I said, "so he was a bit distracted." The lie would throw Ares off the balance. I didn't mind playing on his emotions as he'd intended to fence me in.

A crimson ring formed in his amber eyes, and rage brew in it. "How old were you then?" he asked.

"Twelve."

"That motherfucker molested you when you were only a child?" he asked, the crimson ring deepening and spreading in his eyes.

"Angels are monsters," I said. "Everyone knows that."

"Did you encounter only one Angel at that time?" Einarr asked. Ares was too angry to go on with the next question. Wasn't the advanced human a good sidekick?

Two against one, but one could play a better game.

"I didn't see any others," I said, expecting Einarr to counter me.

"Angels usually hunt in a group of three," said the sidekick.

I frowned. "Do they?"

"According to that bad-eyed Angel, they've been hunting for you in particular," Ares said.

"What's your theory?" I asked, restraining myself from sneering. I still needed to play nice to throw him off my back.

"Why did the Angel call you Princess?" Ares asked, peering into my eye to catch a flicker.

I laughed hoarsely. "You think I'm a princess?"

"No one knows who your parents are," he said.

"They both perished after the Angel War," I said. "I was an orphan. I raised myself in the forest, the one you invaded."

"The Angel wouldn't call you *Princess* for no good reason," Ares insisted.

"Do I look like a princess to you, Your Highness?" I asked. "Would a princess grow up with wolves?" I let humiliation and rage show in my eyes. "That psycho Angel was mocking me."

"There was no mocking in his tone," he said.

"Angels like to call every earthling girl Princess for fun," I said, "especially the ones they tortured and marked to kill."

"I've dealt with Angels for decades, and I've never heard of them calling anyone Princess except you," Ares said. "You said they wanted the First Witch, but he mentioned nothing about her. Who are you really, Freyja, that the whole Angel army will come across the universe for you?"

I wanted to say the Angels had mistaken me for someone else, but that ship had long since sailed. Ares would only think I was hiding something darker.

"So I'm a princess," I snorted. "Enlighten me then, which king and queen are my parents?"

"You tell me," he said.

I threw my hands up, black rage surging in me. "Why are you interrogating me? Why don't you go after the Angels instead of coming after me? Am I such a threat?"

At my outburst, a trace of dark fire crawled up my neck, hissing like a snake.

I darted a panicked, angry look between Ares and Einarr, but none of them seemed to see the fire. Merlin had seen it. I should learn to conjure the fire and turn it into a weapon against the Angels when they came for me again.

At the notion, the dark fire receded. It couldn't be a weapon.

Shame mixing with the need to protect me flashed through Ares' eyes. He turned to Einarr. "Go see to the wounded guardians."

With a nod, Einarr walked off.

"Freyja," Ares softened his voice. "I need to get to the bottom of this so I can better protect you."

I hadn't wanted his trust, so why did I feel hurt and mad that he doubted me? On the other hand, I'd never been honest with him.

My jaw clenched.

"From now on," Ares said, "you'll never leave my side. You'll be my shadow. I move, you move behind me."

"The Angels have marked me," I said. "You and your men will be better off leaving me here. No mortal army can stand the Angel horde."

"We defeated them two decades ago," Ares said. "We drove them away from Earth."

"This time, it will be different," I said. "You have no allies. The Fey Empress and her consort won't come out of their realm. The Dark Lord's Angels want only me. I don't want to put you and your men on the line. You don't need to stick your neck out for me to keep me alive. You'll have other means to find your witch."

"I've decided," he said. "You'll stay with me."

"I can lead the Angels to your precious witch," I said. "Would you rather I endanger her?"

"It won't come to that," he said.

"How do you know, Ares?" I asked incredulously. "You're risking everyone."

"I know what I'm doing," he said. "My instinct says I need to keep you safe at all cost."

"What if I'll be safer without you around me?" I asked.

"Right. The moment you left me, you got three warrior Angels on your hot ass," he said.

"It was actually cold," I said.

Something dark flashed through his eyes. I knew the scene of a naked me perching on top of a screaming Angel had flooded back to him again. I hadn't come up with a plausible explanation for that, and I had no energy for another round of interrogation.

"I'm tired," I said, heading toward a tent that I wanted to claim as mine. "Call me when dinner is ready."

CHAPTER 5

Death Touch

It was too late to withdraw when I realized that the tent belonged to Ares. I should have entered one of the other two tents, but this one was nicer. Since I was the only woman in the group, shouldn't I take the best and have Ares share with his men? It was a logical choice. But throughout the trip, Ares had always shared a room or a suite with me, though not the bed.

I'd figure it out later. Right now, I needed to stay out of Ares' sight, so he wouldn't chase me with more questions. I also needed to relax my muscles after the long ride.

I threw myself onto the bedroll, my feet crossed at the ankles and my hands behind my head, musing on my next move.

"Freyja!" Ares shouted outside the tent. "Come out. I have

a question."

That didn't sound benign. I turned my back to the tent entrance and squeezed shut my eyes to pretend to be asleep.

A few seconds later, footsteps stomped in.

I let my chest rise and fall naturally, slowing my breath until it was even and deep.

Warm breath brushed over my face, pure male scent floated to my nostrils, and electric current charged around me.

"Stop pretending," Ares said through his gritted teeth.

I fluttered open my eyes and gave him a bewildered look. "Did I enter the wrong tent?" I said with a yawn. "I'll go to the other one then."

"You stay here," he said. "But you'll answer my questions truthfully."

"Why must I answer so many questions?" I asked. "Who assigned you to be my interrogator?"

"You, when you attempted to murder me on several occasions," he said mercilessly. All his former tenderness and warmth vanished into the ether.

I stiffened and rose to a sitting position, staring blankly at him.

He'd been brooding when he didn't need to concern himself with my safety and wound. He'd connected some of the dots. I could almost see those dark images flash back and forth in his steely eyes.

The platinum-haired Angel I'd killed had died the same way as the Dragonian and two humans—they all had gray, cracked skin, they all screamed in agony, and they all had trails of smoke burning out of their empty eye sockets.

"How did you kill them, Freyja?" Ares asked.

He already knew. He just wanted me to confess.

"They didn't like my touch," I said, my eyes turning as cold and hard as his.

"Your touch is death," he said, drawing a sharp breath. "That's why you wear gloves all the time."

"Every inch of my skin is lethal," I said. "Not just my hands."

He stared at me, darker storm brewing inside.

"The night we were in Merlin's cabin," he said, "you touched me without knowing I was immune. You wanted me dead."

"I didn't touch you. You gripped my ankle while I tried to get away. I didn't expect you to feign sleep and grab me."

"On several occasions, you marched toward me as you pulled off your gloves with a cold, killing look in your eyes. You would have laid your bare hand on me the first time if Ventus hadn't jumped in front of me to stop you."

That felt like a century ago, and he still remembered that?

"You threatened me," I said, forcing down my guilt, though it kept coming up. "You took me away from my home and my pack. I thought you were going to kill me. I was trying to protect myself."

I stood up, and he mirrored my movement, towering over me.

I inched toward the tent flap, but he blocked it.

"You said you wanted a bath, and then you stripped yourself bare, just like you did with the Angels. You planned to take our lives. If we got into the water with you at that time, you'd have finished us all."

"That was circumstantial," I said, then at his deadly look, I added, "I'm glad no one jumped into the lake. That was a test on your characters, and you all turned out to be better men than I thought."

He wasn't touched by my flattery.

"You meant to slay me. Earth! How could you?" Rage, grief, disbelief and something else exploded in his eyes like a chaotic kaleidoscope.

"I said it was circumstantial." I didn't like to be backed to the corner. "What do you want me to say? Sorry? Would it help?"

"You still have no remorse?" he shouted. "Do you even

have a conscience?"

I pondered his question for a second. I might not have a conscience. I wasn't keen on handling heavy feelings. Guilt could eat at your insides if you let them. Perhaps I was just like my father—a true monster.

"You're still here, right?" I said sheepishly. "As are your men. No harm has been done." I waved my gloved hand at him. "See, I still wear the gloves to protect your men. It's very uncomfortable to wear them all the time, you know."

"I wouldn't be here if I hadn't happened to be immune to your death touch!"

My eyes sparked. That was a new direction we should take. Instead of chasing me and beating me down with my shame and guilt, we should discuss the magical or scientific aspect of his exceptional immunity. At least that way, we could both gain knowledge.

"How?" I asked. "How can you neutralize my touch? Do you think it has anything to do with your enhanced genetic makeup? Isn't it amazing?"

His rage didn't recede, nor was he distracted. He advanced toward me with single-minded menace. I backed toward the other end of the tent since his massive form blocked the only entrance and exit.

"You're a cold, premeditated murderer," he said. "You

tried to kill me while I was sleeping and in cold blood. Earth, you'd have wiped me out that night, and I thought you were hot for me."

"Shush!" I said. "You don't want others to hear that."

The crimson ring in his eyes expanded.

"I almost fell for you," he continued. "I even debated giving up the hunting for the witch and taking you back to Atlantis. I thought of giving us a chance. I almost abandoned all of my dreams and ambitions for you, for a cold-hearted bitch!"

He drew an angelblade strapped on his back.

The blood drained from my face and my heart picked up its rhythm.

I'd backed to the end of the tent.

I threw a hand out before me, hoping my black fire would come out and push him back.

"Is that all you got, wolf girl?" Ares asked, his voice so cold it sent chills down my spine.

Then it dawned on me that dying a swift death today would be better than a slow, agonizing one in two years.

I had nothing to lose. The only thing that plagued me was that I wouldn't get to say goodbye to my pack. But perhaps it was best this way. I wouldn't want to hear their mournful howls.

I pressed my hands against the canvas tent. "Kill me," I said, "if that makes you feel better."

I threw my head back and howled one last time, saying farewell to my pack.

A huge head propelled through the flap, almost bringing down the tent.

"Your Highness," Ventus said, "you don't want to do this. If you kill her, you'll regret it forever!"

"What?" Ares snarled.

"Freyja has her flaws, as you said," Ventus said. "But she isn't a trained warrior."

"This has nothing to do with her training," Ares shouted, the veins on his temples pulsing. "She planned to assassinate me when all I've ever done was defend her."

That wasn't at all how it seemed. Even when I'd considered giving him a taste of my fatal touch, I hadn't really acted on it, or even had had the chance to do it. In the end, he was immune. So what was there to complain about?

Hadn't he said we should move on instead of holding a grudge?

But under the circumstances, I decided not to talk back to enrage him further. I morphed my face into a sad, meek look instead of my usual defiant one, as if I was also sick with myself.

Ares shot me another furious glance. He didn't seem to buy it.

"I won't let you harm Freyja," Ventus said. He brushed Ares away from me, positioning his head between us. Part of the tent was twisted by his effort. "You'll have to get through me to get to her."

My heart warmed. I didn't expect the guardian to show me such loyalty and defend me against his own fearsome master.

"Harm her?" Ares roared. "You think I'll kill her?" But he dropped his gaze and stared at the angelblade in his hand that Ventus and I eyed nervously.

"I drew out the sword for her convenience," Ares said. "I was about to hand it over to her so she could stab it into my heart. She might prefer to stick it in my eye as she did to others—her favorite sport!"

I wanted to say that they were my enemies, but he wasn't. And he was—

My heart ached.

Ares looked at us with disgust. "Although she attempted to slaughter me, I can't harm her. I can never harm her. I can never lay a finger on her."

He swung his sword and hacked at the tent.

"Ares," Ventus pleaded. "Calm down."

"Would you be calm if you were the one she'd tried to

kill?" Ares shouted.

There's a tree outside, Ventus, I said in the guardian's mind. *Advise him to cut it instead of the tent. We can use the branches for campfire.*

Ventus focused on Ares, but he spoke to me, *That will make him madder. Just don't say a word. Let me handle this.*

The way the guardian handled it was to let Ares slash at the tent frenetically. The side near Ares was now sliced open. If he kept at it, soon the whole tent would be a pile of shreds.

The camp became still and quiet. No one dared to take a peek, preferring to stay away from the crazed prince.

I restrained myself from covering my head with my hands in case the tent fell. While Ares assaulted the tent, he kept an eye on me. A tiny movement from me would set him off worse than it already had.

"Let's destroy the damned tree!" Ventus bellowed, baring his fangs at the tree outside the opening torn by the prince.

Ares leapt up toward the tree, his sword chopping at the branches in rage. Twigs fell like hail under his vicious attack.

To encourage his master, Ventus dragged his head out of the flap and bit into the tree trunk.

I debated if I should sneak out of the tent or join them in mangling the tree in an effort to form a new bond. But Ventus sent me a quick, warning glance, so I cowered in the corner.

"Did you see how the Angel died, Ventus?" Ares fumed again as twigs and leaves fell around him. "She intended the same for me."

"I never really wanted you dead, even when you were so mean to me," I said, jogging toward him. "Aren't you still here, showing off your mighty strength?"

Freyja, this isn't the time to be mouthy, Ventus admonished. *Go back to the tent and try to hide from his sight.*

No, I said. *I won't hide. If I stay silent, he'll keep beating me down.*

Ares wheeled toward me, the ring of crimson in his eyes turning darker. Maybe I shouldn't have opened my mouth, but it was too late, so I held my ground and chinned up.

"A moment ago I thought you finally felt some remorse," he gritted. "But you have none. What kind of person are you? How could I even be drawn to someone like you?"

I blinked back the tears that threatened to fall.

"Someone like me?" I spat. "How can I be worse than anyone else? We live in a violent time. People kill for sport. Bad men kill for nothing. You have no idea what they tried to do to me and how they tried to hurt me."

"Who are they?" he snarled, stabbing his sword into the

tree. "Anyone still alive?"

"I was only trying to defend myself," I said. "But what about you, Prince Ares Darken, the great warlord? How many died at your hands in the wars? Thousands? Tens of thousands? Don't piss on me for my efforts at preserving myself. I don't need your lecture on fucking virtues, guilt, or discipline."

Ares glared at me incredulously before narrowing his eyes. "So you regret that you couldn't end me with your death touch? Is that it? Are you thinking of another way to kill me? Like slashing my throat with your sharp angelblade next time I sleep?"

Where did he come up with all the twisted theories? I understood he wasn't exactly reasonable in his fit of rage, but—

"I won't harm you if you don't hurt me," I said.

"When did I ever hurt you?" he asked.

While I tried to search for a few examples, he shook his head with cold contempt. "That's it. I'm done," he said. "I can't even look at you right now. The mere sight of you aggravates me, and your voice makes my stomach churn. I need to get away from you."

He pulled his sword out of the tree trunk and broke into a run, away from me.

In a flash, he was gone.

CHAPTER 6

The Panther

I hunched over the campfire, alone. It was freezing, and I had nowhere to go.

Boomer and Jericko gathered around a bigger campfire to stay away from me. While Ares had shouted at me without discretion, his men had learned about my death touch.

Caen, the silent Dragonian, wasn't in sight this time.

The Dragonian warriors looked at me as if I were a plague. And not just that. Whenever they glanced in my direction, they had that kind of murderous light in their eyes and their hands voluntarily went to the hilt of their swords.

"If Ares hadn't stopped us and we'd gotten into the lake with her that day," Jericko said, "we'd all be cracked pots now."

"I thought she was wild when she stripped bare," Boomer

said. "Never thought the wench was planning our horrific death."

I tried not to hear them and stayed as far away from them as possible. If the guardians weren't around, the bunch would come for my blood.

Einarr was gone, too. Hopefully he'd gone hunting. I wondered if they'd let me have dinner tonight.

Bored and worried, I tried to focus on my next steps.

With so many people having learned about my touch—which was very unfortunate—my skin was no longer my weapon. For the first time, I felt defenseless.

I thought of the dark fire slithering on my skin when I became extremely upset, but I had no idea how to conjure it up and turn it into my new weapon. Merlin had said that I would need to own my heritage, embrace my dark side, and claim my monster if I wanted to become a full-fledged First Witch. Only then could my Angel power be at my disposal.

Maybe I should let the monster out? People already thought I was one. Ares had called me worse. Two monsters together would be stronger than one.

I closed my eyes and withdrew into myself.

I skated on the ice lake toward the spot where I usually checked on my monster.

Shapeless darkness swirled under the ice.

I stared down through the layers of ice, and the darkness transformed into a beast with my face and stared right back at me. I yelped.

I used to call the beast *'he'* to distance myself from it, and now it proved to be a she.

She'd heard my pulses, my heartbeats, and my call.

She'd come to meet me, with the thick ice between us.

She didn't pound on the ice and scream for me to let her out this time. She just looked at me, her crimson eyes half-mad.

I jerked my face away from her, away from my distorted self.

Just like Ares couldn't stand looking at me, I couldn't look her in the eyes.

I fled, my mind returning to my surroundings.

Vast wings flapped overhead and blocked the weak sunlight above. I was grateful and relieved that they weren't the Angels' wings.

Mettalum and Lucas had returned from their scout.

As soon as he landed, Lucas strolled toward me with a smile.

Surrounding by hostility, that sunny smile meant summer to me. I waved and beamed back, welcoming him to join me.

Boomer jogged toward Lucas, and my heart sank. The

Dragonian cut in in front of Lucas halfway. "I wouldn't go near her if I were you, shifter."

My clothing covered every inch of my skin, my gloves were tight on my hands, and my hood concealed most of my face. I wouldn't harm Lucas.

"What's your problem, Boomer?" Lucas growled. "I'm sick and tired of you bullying Freyja. This has to stop!"

Boomer removed himself from Lucas' path. "Well, then, go ahead and touch her and die like the Angel in the alley. You might even prefer smoke coming out of your ass."

That was how people twisted truth. Smoke never came out of the asses of those I touched with death. It came out of their eye sockets.

"What are you talking about?" Lucas said as he flicked a glance in my direction. He'd also seen the corpse of the Angel I'd killed.

"Go ask your sweetheart over there," Boomed said. "Ares almost ran his blade through her for what she intended for us."

Lucas strode toward me but stopped a few feet. I dropped my gaze and stared at his boots. I'd planned his death at the lake, and he'd been nice to me all the time.

"Freyja," he called, squatting in front of me.

"Huh?" I said. I couldn't look him in the eyes.

"I haven't had a chance to talk to you since the Angels' attack," he said. "I hope you feel better now."

"I do, thank you," I said.

"Freyja, you're my friend," he said. "I don't blame you for anything. Even if your touch can cause death, you've been wearing gloves all the time to protect us," he paused and added, "after you got to know us a bit more."

I fought back grateful tears. I would not forget this kindness.

"The love-sick idiot is totally blind," Jericko said with disgust from his campfire. He'd watched our exchange with eager anticipation, hoping Lucas would at least spit on me if not knife me.

I raised my head and looked Lucas straight in the eyes. "I was born with this curse. Everything I touch dies. And it isn't just my hands. Every inch of my skin is lethal."

"I saw the druid touch your hands," he paused, "and one time Ares touched your face."

"Only a few people are immune," I said.

"Maybe I'm immune, too," he said hopefully. "Test me."

"No!" I said in horror. "Merlin gave me a list, and you aren't on it. I'm sorry, Lucas. I didn't mean to hurt you or lie to you."

A hint of sadness crossed his face as he realized what my

words meant, but he put an effort to expel the misery in his eyes. "If I were you," he said, "I wouldn't run around to tell people about the death touch either."

I didn't deserve his kindness.

"Is it curable?" he asked.

"I don't know. I've never tried."

"Do you want to get rid of it?"

I nodded.

"After we find the First Witch," Lucas said, "we'll return to the druid. He must have the cure."

"He doesn't," I said. "But I might find someone else who can cure me."

"Who?" he asked.

I glanced at the Dragonians. They were blatantly eavesdropping. The guardians also pricked their ears. Lucas followed my sight before returning his gaze to me.

"Whoever they are," he said, "I'll go with you to search for them."

He didn't know—none of Ares' men knew—that I was heading toward the Fey realm where the Empress would either cure me or kill me.

"I don't want to put you in danger," I said.

He grinned. "I make love to danger." Then he realized it was too blunt and flushed.

My face flamed.

"Are you sure you have that lethal touch?" he asked, trying to tune it down. "I just can't picture you with death."

Just then, a jaguar charged toward us from the mountain side.

The guardians stirred and rose.

Lucas shifted instantly. A large, black panther now stood between the jaguar and me, growling threateningly.

Caen, who had been missing early on, chased after the jaguar. I wasn't sure if he'd been hunting the animal or driving it toward me by design.

I crouched, tossing my gloves away, and leapt toward the beast.

This was the first time I showed my hunting skills. Like Ares, I could jump high and far. He was genetically enhanced, but I had Angel blood.

I soared across the panther and landed on the jaguar, pressing my hand on its fur. The panther dashed toward us as the jaguar yowled in pain, prone to the ground in fours. I hopped off. The jaguar turned gray, and smoke emitted from its eye sockets.

"End its suffering," I snarled at Caen who had just reached us.

He gave me a dark look and slashed the jaguar across the

neck.

Boomer and Jericko had gathered around the animal, staring at the remaining smoke hovering above the jaguar.

I'd just demonstrated my killing skills. I could have done the same to the group. Jumping on them with one touch, and they would be done for. My show wasn't for them but for Lucas. I didn't want him to get this foolish idea that he could be immune and get himself killed.

Lucas shifted back and stared at me. There was no disgust in his eyes but awe and sorrow. He saw the barrier between us.

I trudged toward my campfire, leaving the group and the dead jaguar behind.

They debated if they could eat the animal since I'd touched it.

All this time, Ventus said, *I thought you were a damsel-in-distress when you climbed onto my back like a frightening fawn. You deceived even the great Guardian of Wind, Witchling.*

For your own good, I said, putting back my gloves.

Ventus snorted.

Fierce as fire, Ignis said, opening an eye to gaze at me.

Cold as ice, said Glacies.

Hard as metal, said Mettalum.

At least, the guardians thought I belonged.

CHAPTER 7

Ice Burn

A sudden commotion woke me up.

The panther rose beside me with a ferocious snarl, fangs bared, ready for a battle.

The shifter had come to sleep beside me to warm me instead of sharing the tent with his team members while I'd curled near the dwindling fire.

I'd protested out of fear of harming him.

"You've covered yourself from head to toe," Lucas had said. "You couldn't harm me even if you want to."

At last, I'd agreed. So I'd slept inside the bedroll while leaning against the large panther, and the mountain air didn't seem that chilly anymore.

"Back off, Lucas," I heard Ares' voice before I saw him towering over us.

What now? I thought wearily. Couldn't he just leave me alone for a night? When had he returned?

Despite my reservations toward him, my pulse quickened at his closeness, and the air crackled with electricity when we shared the space.

"I'm taking Freyja to sleep properly in the tent," Ares said.

Lucas glowered in answer.

When I had first met them, I'd planned to drive a wedge between them, but now I didn't want any of them hurt. If a fight broke out, Lucas would wound Ares, and the prince would kill the shifter.

"It's okay, Lucas," I said, raising my torso and embracing the panther, careful not to let my half exposed face touch him. "I want to sleep in the tent. The hard ground hurts my back."

The panther stopped snarling, calmed by my patting. It was a pity that I couldn't touch him. He'd always been awesome to me, tender and protective but never overbearing. Even after he learned about my death touch, he had still come to keep me warm.

From his brown eyes, I read that he knew how nervous I was sleeping so close to him and how afraid I was to hurt him. But his expression said that he trusted me with his life.

Ares growled threateningly, not like the communication between the panther and me. He grabbed me, scooped me into his arms, and strode toward the tent.

Someone had patched up what Ares had slashed open while I was sleeping.

Over Ares' shoulder, I saw Lucas watching us. He seemed to want to pounce on Ares, but he just stood there, letting Ares carry me into the tent.

I hadn't struggled when Ares had snatched me from Lucas' side because I didn't want any conflict between them, but now that we were alone, I wasn't docile anymore.

"What are you doing?" I demanded, not appreciating being manhandled.

"I want you to sleep on a softer bed," he said.

"Why do you care?"

"You have no idea. I said I'd feed you in the day and get you to a warm bed at night. I'm keeping my promise."

"I chose to sleep on the ground and I was sleeping well," I said.

"I won't risk you falling ill before you find me the witch," he said.

All this protection and consideration was for his witch. I was but the means to the end for him. I was the tool he needed to keep shiny and sharp to work properly.

When he felt like rejecting me, he did that over and over. When he wanted to punish me, he slashed at the tent. When he needed to walk away, he abandoned me right there.

Now when he wanted me near him, he just snatched me from my friend's side. He thought it was his goddamned right to take whatever he desired. I was weary and tired of being pushed around by him.

He wanted me, but he constantly chose another woman who he hadn't met.

There was nothing special about the Dragonian prince. He just happened to be the one that I could touch and feel pleasurable, by the flawed design of the fucking universe.

Believe me, asshole, you'll need more than luck to find the First Witch.

Rage took me, and I swung my arm at him. "Fuck you, and fuck your witch!"

The prince grabbed my wrist. I'd forgotten again how fast he could move, but I didn't give up. I kicked him, and he let me.

I fought back a wince as my foot connected with his shin. It felt like I'd crashed into a boulder.

He frowned at me. "What was that for, Freyja? You fought me because you would prefer to sleep on the hard ground with an animal?"

"How dare you call Lucas an animal?" I said. "How dare you treat me as your property? You kidnapping me doesn't give you the right to lord over me. I don't belong to you and never will. I'm not your fucking slave!"

"How dare I? No one dares to use that word and tone with me," he barked back. "And how dare you be so pissed off while you're the one who have done all the wrong things? I've never treated you as a slave, woman! I even decided to let go of your atrocious attempt at murdering me cold-bloodedly. I even decided to put the past behind us and give you a second chance!"

No one had ever called me *woman* before. It sounded like a big insult when Ares had said it.

"What second chance?"

"We work together like a team again," he said, trying to calm himself.

"Right, I work for you," I sneered. "You still need me to find your witch so you can fuck her and breed a load of brats."

"Freyja, watch your tongue!"

"Once I find her and you don't need me anymore, what will you do to me?" I raised a finger and drew it across my throat. "That's what you'll do. And you'll toss my body in the ocean and feed it to the sharks."

Ares looked at me in horror, then grief-stricken. "That's what you think of me?"

"What else can I think?" I said. "If you'd forgotten I was still useful to you, you'd have cut me instead of the tree today."

The camp was incredibly quiet. Ares and I glared at each other as we realized that everyone was holding their breath and listening. If the tension grew thicker, I was sure Lucas would show up at the tent flap. I wouldn't be able to stop a fatal fight if they got into it again. Lucas was my friend. Despite that Ares was a jerk I didn't want him to get hurt either.

"Go to sleep, Freyja," Ares lowered his voice. "Tomorrow you'll be calmer, and we'll talk if you want. In the meanwhile, I must keep others safe from you and you safe from others. When you stay close to me, it'll be the safest for everyone."

I turned from him, not bothering to send him one last contemptuous look as I crawled into the bedroll and wrapped it tightly around me.

I wanted to be dead to the world tonight and deal with tomorrow's trouble tomorrow.

~

Ice coursed through my veins.

My teeth clattered. My bones numbed.

I had never felt so cold.

I flashed open my eyes. I was breathing frost.

This wasn't normal for me. With potent Angel blood in me, I could sustain extremely low temperatures. I'd proved adaptable in the high air on Ventus' back. Even though mountain's night was chilly, I shouldn't feel like a frozen vegetable.

Cold burned in me.

Then something hit home.

The Fey essence in me had been fighting the dark Angel power within me every now and then, but their struggle had never pushed me to the edge, even as I grew older, the fight between the light and the dark turned fiercer.

It was like the full impact of my curse had just arrived.

But it shouldn't be happening now. It was still a week before my twenty-second birthday.

I clenched my jaw, but it only caused them to grind on each other. I was afraid of waking up Ares and having him question me again, but I couldn't stop the noises.

Ice clogged my veins. Ice burned in my lungs, my throat, and my eyes.

It burned worse than fire.

I muffled a scream, but failed to swallow a pained groan.

Instantly, Ares was at my side. "Were you having a bad dream, Freyja?" he asked.

I couldn't answer. My whole body trembled violently.

"It's okay, I'm here," he said, gathering me into his arms, and my face dropped on his. He pulled me slightly away, eyes widening. "You're like ice, Freyja." He freed a hand and tested my neck, arm, and fingers. "Ice," he confirmed.

The next thing I knew, he was stripping himself bare. "Let me warm you."

He moved inside my icy bedroll and his warrior's body heat was like a small sun. I clung to him like a leech, yet I still shivered from the unquenchable cold.

He started to undressed me. "We'll have to do this so you'll get more heat from me." He left me with only my underwear. His bulge of erection pressed against my icy belly. "I won't do anything. I'll only warm you up."

I wouldn't mind if he wanted to do something. While the cursed ice coursed through my body, the fire of lust also licked at me.

I'd wanted Ares ever since his first touch set me ablaze.

He wrapped around me tightly, and I pressed my freezing, hungry skin against his hot one. Gradually, I stopped trembling as the cold burn receded.

I wouldn't let him go, afraid the ice would return.

He held me for a long time, and I barely moved, not wanting him to pry me off him.

He inhaled my scent deeply before whispering in my ear, "Freyja?"

"Uh?" I answered, my teeth no longer clattering.

"Are you still cold?"

"Yeah."

"But your body is warm now."

"Is it?"

"Don't worry. I'll hold you like this to keep you warm until you fall asleep."

"Only if you want to," I said.

"You can be very sweet when you want to be," he said.

"You think?" I asked. Since I was warm and comfortable, I felt sleepy.

"It hurt me more than anything that you thought I'd harm you," he said. "It hurt more than the truth that you wanted me dead."

I never thought I had the power to hurt his feelings. I thought I was but his means, his trial, his lust, and his prisoner, and nothing more.

"I never wanted you dead," I said. "If I truly wanted you dead, you would be."

"But how could you even think I would kill you?" he asked, his voice ragged.

"You looked frightening. You slashed that long sword in the air like a mad man, and your eyes were red."

"Even so, I would never harm a hair on your head. Couldn't you learn to trust me a bit more?"

"But I'm sleepy now," I said, thankful for his warmth.

"Sleep then," he said. "I'll hold you the whole night." He brushed a kiss on my head.

A strange, tender feeling swelled in my chest.

I pressed my face against his bare chest. I'd wondered how it would feel to have his strong shoulder as a pillow, and now I had it under my head.

His arms tightened around me and his large, hard erection still pressed on my belly. I wouldn't object if he stuck it between my thighs.

Yet neither of us made a move. Only our breath mingled.

"You don't just ask people to trust you," I murmured. Trust was never a free gift.

"What did I do, other than abduct you, to give you the impression that I can't be trusted?"

"You want your witch more than anyone and anything. You'll do whatever it takes to get her. If hurting me is the way to have her, you'll hurt me."

He was silent for a long while, then said quietly, "I've given you a reason not to trust me, but I won't harm you, no matter what."

"Don't promise what you can't deliver, Highness," I said. "I understand why you must do what you do. You have to protect your interest, and the witch is your great interest. As you said, I'm the test you need to pass, the obstacle you need to overcome, to get your final prize—her."

"It isn't like that," he said, then he didn't say anything more. I felt his throat moved as he swallowed hard.

"Sleep," he said. "You'll need your energy tomorrow."

That alarmed me.

"What do I need my energy for if we aren't doing anything tomorrow but waiting for the guardians to recover?"

"We'll be doing something. It'll be our turn to patrol the air. We need to earn our keep."

"Why do I need to earn my keep?" I asked. "I told you I'm not your soldier. My sole function is to lead you to the witch. You can't assign me other errands to wear me out."

He laughed. "Sleep, Freyja. We'll talk tomorrow."

"The better you understand this, the better we'll get along," I said. "I don't owe you, but you owe me big time by dragging me out of my comfortable home to find your future. So it's your priority to keep me safe, warm, and nourished, and then I'll be able to perform and find your witch."

"Isn't this what I'm doing," he said, tugging me closer, "to keep you warm?"

I complained a bit more to make sure he understood me before sleep took me in its sweet warm, dark nest.

CHAPTER 8

Fire Burn

When I woke up in the morning, Ares wasn't in the tent, but his warmth and scent lingered. I inhaled, half-closing my eyes, remembering what had transpired yesterday.

Ice had burned in my veins, and Ares had expelled the cursed cold with his body heat. His touch had not only brought out the ravenous lust in me; it could also heal me. With his aide, I awoke with such vigor.

Lying alone half-naked in the bedroll, I missed the prince's presence. I was warm now, but I had another need for him. I inserted my fingers into my panties and brushed my sex. It was hot and wet with aching want.

Then I heard voices outside the tent. My hearing wasn't as superior as an Angel's, but it was sharper than any other earthling species. I pricked my ear and concentrated. Ares was conversing with Caen behind the tree that he'd hacked yesterday.

"What's going on, Ares?" the no-longer-silent Dragonian asked. "You've never acted jealous before when it came to women. You were always casual and you were never territorial. What's so special about this wolf girl?"

Ares warned, "Careful, cousin."

Cousin? Caen was Ares' royal cousin?

"You almost twisted off the shifter's head last night," his cousin said. "You'd never fought your men over a woman, regarding it beneath you. But ever since you brought this wolf girl along, you've been acting like a virgin boy under her spell."

"I'm not a virgin boy," Ares snapped. "And she has a name."

"Have you slept with her?" his cousin asked.

"That's none of your business," Ares snarled.

"If you sleep with her, you throw away everything you've worked so hard for." Now that Caen had opened his mouth, he wouldn't stop. "Your fealty is to the First Witch," he continued. "If you aren't faithful to her, you'll lose your perfect mate and true queen. Have you forgotten the Oracle's words—only the First Witch will bring you the greatest kingdom Earth has ever seen and produce superior offspring that no other race could compete with?"

My heart sank. No wonder Ares desired the witch more than anyone. Which man on Earth could turn that down? It wasn't a temptation. It was an irresistible promise.

"I haven't slept with Freyja," Ares said.

I bet he was proud of himself. He would have hated both of us if he had acted on his lust for me last night.

Caen blew out a relieved breath.

"Maybe I don't want the great kingdom," Ares said in a dejected voice. "Maybe I'm no longer that ambitious."

My heart stuttered.

"Did you hear what you just said, Ares?" Caen demanded. "If you think with your dick, you'll also lose Atlantis. Your father's kingdom will be divided and there will be a civil war. Your pure-bred brothers have considerable supporters. Many won't follow a half-blood heir after you father is gone, unless you bring them a new prospect. Only when you secure the First Witch, and she shows her great, terrifying power and gives you a superior heir and children, it will convince our race that your father's idea of the hybrids and super species is indeed the future of our people. Only then, will your rule never be contested again."

The Dragonians placed such a burden on the First Witch—she had to bring Prince Darken a grandeur kingdom on Earth, breed super-race children for him, and display her terrifying power in front of the entire nation to convince them.

What woman in her sane mind would want that?

I was so glad that they only knew me as the wolf girl, who was supposed to be wild, free, and irresponsible. Good luck finding the witch. Let them chase their own tails.

I sat up and thanked Goddess Rhea that this bunch would never, ever, connect me to the witch.

But why had the Oracle sent Ares to me?

Merlin had also said I would be a great queen.

Give me a break.

After what I'd heard today, I would rather not claim the she-beast at the bottom of the lake and demonstrate a forbidden, terrifying power.

I would bring chains to myself being the First Witch.

I would be free forever being a wolf girl, until the day I expired.

I would shove the "greatness" up anyone's ass but mine.

I dressed myself and stretched a bit as I continued eavesdropping. The duo was basically whispering. They didn't think anyone could hear them.

Good thing they kept underestimating me.

"The witch is your future," Caen said. "What can Freyja offer you? Sure, she's a wild beauty, but you've had so many beautiful women in your bed that you lost count. None of them even left an impression. Perhaps the wolf girl is different—I've never seen you look at any other women the way you look at her, but this infatuation will pass. No matter how special she is to you right now, she isn't the great First Witch. Only your fated mate will bear your offspring and share your throne. If you screw the girl, you'll lose everything. If she becomes the threat to your future and your kingdom and you don't have the heart to take her out, I'll do it for you."

I heard a ferocious snarl from Ares, then a gagging sound from his cousin.

"I don't care how loyal you are to me," Ares said, the brutality in his voice making me shudder. "I don't care that you're my first cousin. And I don't give a damn that you'll do everything to help me secure my rule. But if you lay a finger on or have anyone touch Freyja—I swear on my mother's grave—I'll erase you and your entire house from the face of the Earth."

Indecipherable noises followed Ares' words. It seemed that Ares had let go of Caen.

"I won't harm the girl," Caen said after he stopped coughing. "But you need to let her go. She's wrong for you in every way."

"I appreciate your concern," Ares said. "How I deal with Freyja is my own fucking business."

"I won't say it again," Caen said. "In the end you'll have to choose: living with nothing with the wolf girl or living with the witch who can give you everything."

I strode toward them like I owned the mountains. They snapped their heads at me. Caen's gaze on me darkened, but Ares' only brightened. I wasn't wearing the cloak that usually concealed my face and I hadn't put on my gloves.

"Ares," I asked, bracing hands on my hips, "where's the breakfast?"

~

Ares hadn't been joking last night when he'd said we would be on patrol today.

"Why do you need me for this, Prince Darken?" I asked, standing several feet away from Ventus and refusing to get on his back. "I'm not a scout and I don't like chores."

The main reason I didn't want to go was because I was afraid of being spotted by the Angels. Eye-patch might have brought more of his pals to look for me. The Dark Lord had seen me through the link. His charcoal eyes had stared back at me like an endless pit, making me shudder with chills. His legion could be upon Earth anytime now.

"What did I say about earning a keep last night?" Ares said. "And I've just fed you."

"I don't care about earning my keep," I said. "Why don't you just throw me out?"

Ares stalked toward me. "Wherever I go, you go. I lead, you follow. It should always be that way."

"Who says so?" I said as I backed away from him. "All my life I've followed no one. I'm not going to start now."

Ares growled.

"Freyja, I have a proposal," Ventus said. He watched our argument with a keen interest. Wild wind was in his nature. He didn't like harmony. He thrived from chaos.

"That's not completely true," the guardian frowned at me. "I'm only thinking of your benefit this time. You can either go see the spectacular view of the war zone with the prince and me or stay here let your Dragonian nemeses glare at you the entire day. They won't cook you lunch."

Einarr wasn't around. The three Dragonians might scheme to kill me. Caen had proposed to take me out this morning. And I had no lethal weapon against them since they now all knew about my death touch.

"What war zone?" I asked.

"Humans are fighting Kinnaras on the other side of the mountains we'll have to cross," Ares said, regarding the spark in my eyes before turning to Ventus. "Let's go without her. We invited her for a grand view, and she thought it a chore." He no longer advanced toward me, but strode back to the guardian.

"Wait!" I called, chasing after him. "Do you mean centaurs?"

"Yeah," he said in a bored tone. "The half-man half-horse species."

"I've never seen a centaur before," I said. "I'll go patrol with you."

"You aren't needed anymore," he said. "Actually, you're dismissed. I can't allow you to keep nagging—"

I ran past Ares toward Ventus.

Ares had always lifted me and placed me on the guardian's back in the past when I'd pretended to be fragile. Now that everyone knew my lethal secret, there was no need for any pretense.

I broke into a run and leapt. Effortlessly and gracefully, I landed on Ventus' massive shoulder.

You should have giving me a fair warning, Witchling, Ventus said.

I thought you preferred my dramatic entrances, I said.

Yeah, well, he said.

I settled on the seat and turned to give Ares a victorious

look.

Everyone dropped their jaws, amazed at the height I could jump to. Only Lucas wasn't around. I guessed he was still upset with Ares.

Ares looked at me, a golden light sparkled in his eyes, and there was undisguised desire in them. A pair of tiny wings did a funny flutter in my stomach. Now I was really looking forward to patrolling with him. I hoped he'd slide his strong arm around my waist when we were in the air.

I'd slept on his warm chest last night and I still couldn't get enough of him.

This feeling was more dangerous than pure lust. I wanted to fuck him, but I had no intention of falling for him. It'd be a miserable business to fall for the future ruler of Atlantis.

Ares shook his head. "If you want her to go one direction, all you need is to point to the other."

He thought he'd figured me out, didn't he?

Ventus flapped his vast, taloned wings and surged to the air. At the same time, Ares leapt, like an arrow, and sat behind me.

Did he always have to outshine me?

Ventus took us sailing across the snowy mountains.

He flew low and with leisure. I looked down at the multitude of white mountains sprawled beneath me and didn't swat at the arm Ares snaked around my waist. He took it as a sign of encouragement and leaned into me to inhale my scent, his face almost buried in my neck.

Even his breath on my skin could bring me shivers of pleasure. I enjoyed it for a few more seconds before turning to scowl at him. "Why are you sniffing at me?"

"I was curious what kind of soap you used," he said. "It smells—interesting."

"What do you mean, interesting?" I asked, annoyed. "It's either good or bad. Interesting doesn't say anything."

He laughed. "It says something, and it's interesting."

Ventus also chuckled. *It's interesting*, he said in my head.

"You didn't bring any soap, so what could I use? And I didn't get to bathe last night, unless you wanted me to freeze my ass off."

He'd warmed me the whole night while I had only my undergarments. I also remembered the feel of his large, hard erection against my belly.

"Einarr bought all the toiletries you'd need," Ares said lazily. "You should ask him."

"Last time I asked, and you said—" I stopped. When I had bathed in the lake and asked him kindly to fetch me a soap, he'd said he and his team weren't pussies that carried soap.

"Perhaps this is your natural smell?" he asked, his nose

brushing my neck, as if he couldn't get enough of my aroma.

To show my generosity, I let him sniff me.

Enveloped by his scent that reeked of territorial male and protectiveness, my fear of the Angels dissipated. I relaxed against him, watching the sunlight sparkle off a ridge of snow-capped mountains and the guardian's scales.

Ventus glided through the landscape.

It was all like a beautiful dream.

Ares hadn't brought up his precious witch much since he'd rescued me from the Angels. Before, he had constantly mentioned her with reverence. Now he seemed unwilling to get into the topic about her. It didn't matter. We'd still be going in the direction he thought he would meet her.

You don't know much about men, do you, Witchling? Ventus said in my head.

I know enough about men, I hissed.

Then you should know about his feelings for you, Ventus said. *He got you to patrol with him in order to spend time with you alone.*

We aren't alone, I said. *You're here, listening to our every chat and intervening whenever you feel like.*

I'm not the third wheel, Ventus said in annoyance. *Anyway, the prince thinks about you all the time.*

Like you can read a man's mind and heart, I snorted.

You're all open books to me, Ventus said.

Really? I said. *Read me.*

The guardian tried to brush my mind, and I shoved and punched him.

Ouch! Ventus cried. *You're being difficult. But the prince's mind has no shield. As a red-blooded hybrid Dragonian male, he thinks you have the loveliest body he's ever seen. He relishes his every touch on it.*

I blushed furiously. *Ventus, that's private.*

Not to me, Ventus lazily blew out a stream of wind. *I think we should probably end this game. It's best you just tell him you're the witch, so we can all go home. The Angels are hunting you. The prince will protect you with his great army in Atlantis.*

I didn't want to hurt his feelings by telling him that none of Atlantis' army and his brethren could hold against the coming Angel legion. At some point, I would have to ditch all of them and go my own way. If I was lucky, I would reach Mysth in time. If I didn't, there was no need to drag down the whole party with me.

I wasn't being sentimental. I was merely practical.

It's getting harder to keep your secret identity at all times, Ventus complained.

I can't tell him. It's complicated, I said. *And you won't tell him a thing either.*

How can it be complicated? Ventus asked. *I've never seen him want any woman like he wants you. Though his mind is slow to realize it due to your deception, his primal male instinct has recognized his mate.*

Stop, Ventus!

You're putting both of you through unnecessary torture, Ventus said.

When did you become a relationship expert? I retorted.

He wants you so much that he hates himself for it. He hates himself for not being able to be faithful to his future mate.

You've just said it, I said coldly. *Ares doesn't want me more than anyone. He wants the witch more than anyone.*

But the witch and you are one and the same!

Not the same in his head! I said. *He'll choose her over me any second of the day. I understand his reason. The Oracle promised him that she would give him everything. No sane man would turn that down. But it isn't because I'm bitter or vindictive that I won't tell him who I am. Ares and I won't have a future together. If he knows I'm the witch, he'll be disappointed beyond consolation. He pictures her as his perfect mate and regards her as a goddess. Even if he finally accepts me as the witch, he'll only lose me eventually. So you'll zip your big mouth instead of meddling and breaking his heart.*

What? Ventus asked. *You lost me. What do you mean you two aren't a perfect match? No one else can be more perfect for him. And how can he lose you?*

No matter how close you are to him, Ventus, I sighed. *The prince doesn't think like you. He won't want a woman just for love or lust. He'll be the ruler of Atlantis. He'll be the new Commander, a Dragonian king. He's chasing the First Witch for the kingdom and many other benefits she'll bring him.*

You can do that, Ventus said.

I've been living on borrowed time, I said. *My curse caught up with me last night. It'll only get worse. I thought I had two years, but I was wrong. I don't have much time.*

What curse, Freyja? Ventus asked. His whole body tensed beneath me.

"Freyja," Ares called, pulling me tightly against him, not liking the space between us.

"What?" I asked.

"I wonder what it means that I'm the only man who can touch you," he said.

"You aren't the only one," I said, turning to look at him cheerfully.

He frowned at me. "Who else?" Then a light of delight sparked in his amber eyes. "Any man who touches you dies a painful death."

"Have you forgotten Merlin can also touch me?" I asked. "You aren't all that special, Prince."

"The druid has a magical shield," he said. "I'm but a normal man."

"You're genetically enhanced."

"The guardians are also genetically-enhanced, intelligent, super beings," Ares said. "But I doubt they can sustain your touch. Not that I encourage you to try on them."

"My touch will harm them," I admitted.

"That's what I meant," said Ares. "There's a reason behind my immunity to your lethal touch."

"There's no special reason behind it whatsoever," I insisted. "Merlin can touch me like a normal man as well. He didn't put up his magical shield when he held my hands in his."

A threatening grunt rumbled from Ares' chest, and his dark eyes flashed displeasure. "He had no business holding your hands. Anyway, he's far away. We won't see him again."

"I want to see him again," I said. "If all goes well, my pack and I can live with Merlin after this is over."

"You and your pack will live in my Atlantis palace," Ares said, yet he didn't mention how we were going to live with the witch.

"We'll pass," I said.

Ares growled. "No normal, sane woman would turn down my offer."

Such arrogance.

"I'm not a normal woman," I said. "I'm a wolf girl. Plus, Merlin has more to offer. He's single, handsome, and powerful. He's a king in his own rights. He can touch me just fine. He might even need a queen."

Hadn't Merlin said that I would be the queen to a great nation?

Though my interest in the druid was merely magical, I wasn't going to explain that to Ares.

"You won't go see him," Ares said. "You'll stay with me so I can protect you. You still have Angel hunters on your tail. Merlin is only one man, but I have a great army."

"What will your witch think if I live in your palace?"

He paused, and Ventus held his breath, dying to know the answer as well.

"I think she'll understand," he said quietly, almost sadly.

I didn't want to see him sad.

"Ventus," I said, "you fly like an old man. Get us to the

war zone so I can see the centaurs. I hope they're drop-dead gorgeous and make my heart flutter."

Ares growled again. Why was he jealous when all he wanted was the witch?

Ventus sped up and left the snowy mountains behind, and I sang a farewell song to Ventus in the native Earth tongue.

Ares rubbed his chin over my head. "Why are you singing a sad song, Freyja?" he asked tenderly. "You never told me about your parents. Who are they? How did you get this death touch? Tell me and I can help you. I helped you last night, didn't I? I warmed your bed. Who are you really, Freyja?"

"I'm the First Witch," I said.

Ventus plunged a hundred feet from the air as if he suddenly forgot how to fly.

"Sure," Ares said, "and I'm the Dark Lord of All Angels."

Ares would only call me delusional if I told him that the ancient, powerful being was actually my grandfather, who was sending his legion to come after me as we spoke.

See, I told him. He didn't believe me, I said in Ventus' head. *You don't need to feel guilty for not ratting me out. Even if one day he learns the truth, he can't blame you.*

"Ares," Ventus called.

I forbid you, I said with a command voice and the

guardian startled, as was I.

My magic—the dark fire on my skin, the wind that had snuffed out Merlin's spear of fire, and my power voice—had popped out now and then like sparks. But I had no control over it and no idea where to begin with.

If I could master my power, I wouldn't be so worried about the Angel legion.

"Centaurs!" I cried in delight.

Beneath us, on the broad plains, two armies opposed each other. Humans on horses and on foot, carrying long spears and daggers; Proud centaurs, who had a man's head and upper torso and a horse's lower body and hooves, stood tall with their bows and axes.

"Are they magical beings?" I asked.

"They wield no magic," said Ares. "They aren't like the Fey. They aren't like any species."

"Can we drop lower so I can see the guys better?" I asked Ventus.

"No," Ares said. "It's dangerous."

The centaurs were fascinating to watch until an archer spotted us and sent an arrow flying toward us.

"Dick!" I shouted.

Ares shattered the arrow with his ray gun, before it could scratch the thick scales on the guardian's body. I approved when Ares shot the archer in retaliation.

The centaurs blew the horns, and humans beat the drums in response. Two bloodthirsty armies charged toward each other with battle cries, thrusting their spears before them and raising their axes.

Thousands of arrows flew toward the other sides.

Earth was such a violent planet. Unlike my mother, I wouldn't sacrifice myself for these species.

"Get us out of here, Ventus," Ares ordered. "Freyja is done with sightseeing."

His arm wrapped around me to shield me; his other hand trained the ray gun toward the ground, ready to take out any threat. Ventus was vigilant as well.

"We just got here," I said.

"Any of the flying arrows can hurt you," Ares snapped.

"But we're so high in the air," I said.

"I'm not taking any chance with you around," he said.

I wanted to watch the war. I wanted to learn to fight a war since I would face one soon.

"I'm not made of a glass," I said.

"You *are* to me," he said.

I turned to glare at him. Overbearing—

"Should we worry about the humans' aggression, Your Highness?" Ventus asked. "They breed so fast. They've taken one-third of the continents."

"Not yet," said Ares. "While they're still engaged in primary warfare."

Despite the humans' speedy evolution, the Dragonians remained the technologically dominant race. I guessed Ares wasn't too concerned since he held onto the Oracle's promise—the First Witch would give him a superior offspring.

Did I look like one who would give birth to a super race?

I almost laughed at the irony, but then I thought of Ares' touch. I thought of sleeping in his arms. My skin was starved for his every stroke. My body, even now, was on fire in his embrace.

"Should we go this route tomorrow?" the guardian asked.

"We'll make a detour," Ares said. "Anything can happen in the war zone. Besides, we're in no hurry to reach south."

In no hurry? Now he wasn't in a hurry to meet the witch. But I needed to get to Mysth as soon as possible. The curse had hit me badly last night. It would only get worse and more frequent. I couldn't afford to be delayed.

"Why must we detour?" I asked. "We'll fly high and straight toward south."

"The war zone can attract the Angels," Ares said.

"They can be anywhere. That's why we need to push

harder toward south," I said.

"Is there anything you haven't told me about since you're in such a hurry?" Ares asked.

"Don't you want to meet your witch sooner?" I said.

"I know your plan," Ares grated. "You can't wait to get rid of me."

This was ridiculous. He was the one who had been in desperate search of the witch.

"I hope this time you won't lead me to another fake witch," he added.

When had he become so unreasonable? I asked Ventus. *Has he always been like that?*

Congratulations, Witchling, said Ventus as he made a sharp turn and headed back toward the mountains. *You've succeeded in messing him up. He can no longer think straight around you.*

Then I felt the first spark of fire flickering in my veins. Ice had hit me last night, and fire was coming.

Ventus, I called, *could you fly at maximum speed? I don't feel good.*

What do you mean you don't feel good, Freyja? Ventus asked in concern.

Go as fast as you can, please, I said. *And fly as low as possible. I'm burning.*

When the fire burst out, I would have to jump so I wouldn't hurt Ares and Ventus.

As the guardian shot out like lightning, a strong current hit me in the face, yet the wind couldn't cool my body temperature.

"Why do you have to go so fast, Ventus?" Ares asked.

"Freyja is burning up," Ventus said, pushing his speed limit.

Everything became hazy beneath us.

"Burning up? How?" Ares asked, pressing his hand against my face. "You're warm. You have a fever." He shouted, "Speed up, Ventus!" As if the guardian could go any faster.

Sparks of fire soared in me. I was sure it would erupt out of my mouth.

The camp was now right beneath us. The three guardians hunched at the foot of the snowy mountain, napping. Ares' royal cousin was studying the runes on his broad angelblade. Boomer and Jericko were parrying, crossing blades.

Lucas looked up as we approached, and Einarr stood beside him, conversing with him.

From ten feet high, I leapt from Ventus' back.

"Freyja!" Ares shouted. "What are you doing? You're going to hurt yourself!"

He jumped right after me. While I fell on the apex of his men's tent, he landed by it.

Fire burst out of my skin and lit the tent.

At least, I hadn't hurt Ares and Ventus. I counted that as a lucky break.

I tumbled down from the tent, and my clothes were on fire. I screamed as I tried to tear them off, but they already burned to ashes. I watched myself turn into a human torch in horror and hurled toward the snowy ground at the base of the mountain.

"Freyja!" Ares chased after me and roared. "What's happening? Put out the fire! Help her!"

Everyone dashed toward me, yelling something.

I threw a burning hand out to fend them off. "Stay . . . away!" I shouted. "Touch me and . . . you'll all burn."

The fire in me grew hotter. The fucking Fey essence and the dark Angel power battled fiercely inside me.

I howled in agony and rolled in the snow, hoping the ice could put out the flame.

A blast of icy wind slammed into me, sending me crashing against a row of rocks.

"Careful, Glacies!" Ares yelled at the ice guardian. "She isn't built like you."

"Only ice can help her now," Glacies said.

It didn't. It couldn't.

The bright red and orange flame engulfed me.

Fire sizzled in my hair, yet it didn't singe a single strand. It only hurt like the inferno from the seventh hell. The curse refused to show me mercy with a quick death.

Glacies kept aiding me with his icy wind, but to no avail. Neither could the snow cool my skin. Then someone poured ice water over my head while I was on all fours, crawling and writhing in anguish.

The fire hissed and leapt higher as if fueled.

"It didn't work!" Ares shouted in a blind panic.

"Anything you do," I cried, "will make it worse."

I howled more, alone in the burning hell.

Ares' face twisted in agony, as if he also lived in my hell.

For the first time, the Dragonians didn't mock me but stared at me in incomprehensive horror.

Einarr got a blanket in his hand, but my fire leapt to it and burned it.

Lucas shifted, trying to get to me in his panther form.

"Don't, Lucas!" I called. "I'll burn … you. It will burn … you."

The large, black panther still tried to get near me, but the flame crashed into him and lit a patch of his beautiful shining fur. The panther staggered back, bellowing in pain. Glacies turned his ice on the shifter and snuffed out the fire.

At least the guardian's ice could put out the fire on the others.

"Sorry, Luca—" I choked, throwing my hands to my throat as the flame seared through my airway.

Ares lunged at me, but the Dragonian warriors caught him and held him back. He struggled free. "Freyja, tell me what to do," he called. "I'll do anything!"

"Maybe it's the venom from the angelblade," Einarr said.

"It's my … curse."

"What curse?"

"Ice in my … veins; fire … in my blood," I gasped. "It's supposed to hit me … at a full force … after I reach … my twenty-second birthday. It came a week earlier." I crawled, sinking my fingernails into the dirt and scratching the rocks as fire burned away the snow, as fire roasted my inner organs.

Fire even burned away the blood on my fingers.

Something registered in Ares' eyes. He'd seen me breathing frost. Last night it was ice, and today flame.

"We must get her to the druid!" Ares ordered.

"We can't move her," Ventus said. "We can't touch her."

"What about Ignis?" Ares asked. "He's fire. Fire won't burn fire."

"My fire … will burn him," I said through my gritted teeth.

I couldn't hold any longer.

"Go with Einarr to fetch Merlin," Ares barked at Ventus.

"Merlin knows my curse," I sobbed. "Only the Fey Empress can cure me."

That posed a dilemma. They couldn't move this human torch. Even if they reached the Twilight Realm and had the slim luck to convince Empress Rose to come for me, I'd be a pile of ashes when she got here.

Staring into Ares' devastated eyes, I knew he had thought of the same thing.

"Freyja," he said, tears streaming down his face. "There must be a way to put out the damn fire."

It was boiling every inch of my lethal skin.

"End me," I pleaded. "I have no more than a year left anyway. End me now!"

If I lived from this moment on, I'd be living in pure hell, afraid of the return of the curse of fire and ice, afraid of being hunted and caught by the Angels, and afraid of bringing death to Ares, Lucas, the guardians, and even the Dragonians.

And if my grandfather got his hands on me, he would shatter my soul to pieces. He would devour and digest every shredded essence of mine. I would feel the agony worse than I was experiencing now. That was his process of draining my power.

If the Dark Lord returned to his power, the universe would sink into a new dark age.

Taking me out would be doing a great service to all living things.

"If you don't have it in you to do it," I snarled, "toss me an angelblade."

I might not have enough strength to stab the dagger all the way into my heart. I'd opt to slash my throat when I received his gift.

I preferred Ares or his men do it for me, but since they had no guts to carry on . . .

"No," Ares said. "I can't. We'll find a way, Freyja. You must live. Please. Just give me a little more time. I'm thinking hard. We'll find a way, Freyja! You must keep being brave."

Brave, my butt!

I bellowed at a new wave of agony and dragged myself toward Caen and an angelblade strapped at his thigh. He wanted me gone, so I wouldn't stand between his prince and the witch queen. He would be more than happy to give me the dagger and let me end myself.

I kept crawling on all fours toward Caen, every inch an effort in hell. Flames lit me, whooshing in the wind. A few more steps and I would reach him.

But that motherfucker jumped back from me.

Though he wanted to, Caen wouldn't give me the dagger. For he knew if he did, Ares would knife him and his entire household.

"Give me the fucking blade!" I howled.

"Freyja, hang in there, please," Ares begged, his eyes bloodshot. I wondered if he ever begged anyone else in his life. "There's a way to save you. There must be a way."

I turned to Ares. "Will you let me suffer like this? End me. You can find your witch another way . . . the Oracle will tell you."

Pain. Burning. Endless agony. I cursed the day I was born.

I cursed the Angel King, my father, to the ultimate eleventh hell!

"To hell with the witch," Ares called. "I want you alive, not for her! I can't bear—" With a roar, he threw away the two Dragonians who held him in place and lunged at me again, but Caen got him just in time to trip him. They both fell to the ground and wrestled. The rest of the Dragonians jumped on him to pin him down.

"She's not your witch!" his cousin yelled.

Roaring in fury, Ares threw them off him with explosive strength and came for me.

"Stay away!" I edged back from him, but Ares had flung himself on top of me, using his body to extinguish the fire.

The flame spread to him and he cried in pain.

I tried to shake him off to preserve him, but I could barely move.

"Don't do this, Ares," I begged. "Leave me."

"Never leave you," he said and pulled me into his arms.

While I was burning in the living hell, my body still craved his touch.

"I can't stand seeing you burn," he said, clenching his teeth and suffering the scorching fire. "Let me burn with you." And he slanted his mouth over mine.

The fire swallowed us both.

CHAPTER 9

Lust Burn

The flame leapt between our lips, yet Ares kept kissing me.

His hunger for me became hotter than the flame.

When his tongue urged my lips open, I obliged, and it thrust into my mouth, turning into another kind of fire that excited me instead of harming me.

I should let him go—he could still be saved, but I was too selfish to do so. When he touched me and desired me like this, the cursed fire no longer hurt.

My hand clutched at his face.

Ares had no intention of getting away. He deepened his kiss, and the cursed fire winked out of my skin, then my hair, and my body.

The burning was gone, replaced by another kind of arousing burn that needed to be sated and cooled as well.

My tongue danced with his. A deep groan rose from the back of his throat. Ares scooped me up.

His mouth left me, and I protested.

Ares pressed me tightly against him as he strode toward his tent.

"Amazing!" Ventus called behind us. "Did you see that? Our prince tamed Freyja's hellfire with a kiss."

"I feel like crying," Glacies said. "I probably shouldn't. Ice is my nature."

"Passion burns as fire," Ignis sighed. "Only it's now a different kind of fire."

They were all very mouthy, but I was grateful for their support.

At the entrance of the tent, Ares stopped and turned to look at the guardians. "No one comes in."

"Yes, Your Highness." Ventus nodded. "Let me know if Freyja needs anything else. I'll even pluck the stars for her."

"It's not your role to pluck the stars for her," Ares growled. "It's mine." He flapped the tent open and entered with me in his arms.

Gently, he laid me down on the bedroll, but I refused to release my arms that coiled around his neck, afraid of the return of the cursed fire if I let go of him.

"It's okay," he said, his voice still choked. "I'm here. I

won't let you burn again."

I didn't unclasp my hands.

"Didn't I melt the ice in your vein and cool the fire in your blood?" he asked. "You need to learn to trust me a little more."

I still hesitated.

"I need to check on you," he coaxed. "And then I'll touch you all over."

My eyes shone at the promise. I loosened my hands and allowed him to place me on bed.

He examined my body carefully. "There are no physical burns or blisters. Your skin is returning to its creamy color." He turned me around to inspect further. After he was done, he gathered me into his arms again.

"How do you feel now, Freyja?" he asked. "Tell me honestly."

I frowned. "When wasn't I being honest?"

"Good. Now that your attitude is back, you're back to normal."

As pieces of my senses returned, the image of him throwing himself at the fire on me flooded back. He would rather burn with me than see me burn alone. My fire had scorched him in the beginning before vanishing.

I touched his face, then his neck, and then his muscled

arm. "You're not hurt, Ares," I said with amazement and gratitude. "But I saw my cursed fire burn you when you jumped on me. Why did you do that? You could have gotten yourself killed."

"I'm the only man who is immune to both your death touch and cursed fire," he said, a smug satisfaction lighting his eyes. "I wonder why."

Because you might be my mate, and my instinct would never hurt my mate, just like your instinct is to always protect me.

"Thank you," I said, gazing at him with tenderness I hadn't known I possessed.

He gazed back at me, his throat moving up and down.

"Don't do this to me again," he said in a shaky voice. "Two days ago, I had to watch the enemy's blade cut into your skin. Today I watched you burn and could do nothing about it. I'd never felt so helpless and powerless."

"You're the opposite of powerless, Prince Ares Darken," I said. "As you bragged, you warmed my ice and cooled my fire. And fates! My touch is death, but yours is electricity. It energizes me."

Was I telling him too much?

"I hadn't known fear until I realized I could lose you," he said, burying his face in the curve between my neck and shoulder blade. He started to inhale my scent, wanting some comfort. And then before I knew it, his hot lips were on my neck, tracing up until they found my mouth.

He laced his large hand into the thickness of my hair, holding the back of my skull firmly as his kiss weighed on me. It was a commanding kiss that didn't allow to be denied or be brushed off. I had my own demands. The tip of my tongue licked his lips and urged them to open, and when they did, I thrust my tongue into his delicious mouth, laying on his before flirting, teasing, and dancing with it.

A stream of energy zipped in me, washing away my exhaustion. It seemed we both got a good deal. When I touched him, I didn't drain him but offered some stimulation, and when he fondled me, he juiced me up. Prince Ares Darken was my energy bar.

A deep, erotic groan tore from the depth of his throat, and his other hand cupped my breast hard.

Lust flooded me, and liquid fire licked between my thighs and spread beyond.

I broke the kiss to get some air into my lungs. "Ares," I breathed.

"I promised you I would have your breast in my mouth. I'm going to fulfill it now." He lowered his head, and his mouth was on my breast. It traveled a short distance until it found my taut nipple. His large, rough hand moved away from my other breast down to my flat belly, then further down. His palm held my bottom and his thumb caressed my clitoris.

I swayed my hips and moaned. The pleasure was going to undo me.

He lifted his head and gazed into my lust-filled eyes, his desire burning brightly and darkly. "Freyja," he whispered, his sensual lips now tracing all the way down, every kiss making me shiver with need.

Then his face was between my thighs.

His mouth enveloped my folds and suckled my tender flesh. His gentleness turned savage.

Pleasant sensations hit me like wild lightning. I bucked my hips up.

"You smell better than anything, my Freyja, and your taste is like no other," he said, his wicked tongue flicking my moistened mound, licking and tasting.

I moaned as pleasure hit me wave after wave. I raised my torso and curled my fingers into his hair. He thrust his pointed tongue into my tight, heated channel.

"Oh, Ares!" I cried.

"Do you want more?"

"Please!"

"My tongue or my cock?" he asked.

Why did he always ask me tough questions?

"Your tongue and your cock," I breathed.

"You can only have one at a time," he said, lust slurring his voice.

"I want your cock."

"Ready to be fucked?"

I lifted my hips up and let my bare pussy show him how eager I was.

"Don't you want this?" I whispered.

He let out an erotic groan. "You have no idea how I fantasized to fuck you every morning when I woke up and every night before I slept. I wanted to take you the first time I laid my eyes on you. I'm forever hard when you're around."

"Then what are you waiting for?" I purred.

In a flash, he stripped off his clothes, baring his broad shoulders, hard chest, narrow waist, and powerful legs. Earth, the prince was magnificent. I had to have him. And I was going to have him! His large cock erected proudly above my face. It was pure male, silky and beautiful. A moist bead surfaced at the slit of his crown, which displayed just how much he wanted me.

I swallowed, imagining how it would feel when his cock filled me, though I'd had it inside me for a brief time before.

"Say 'Ares Darken, I want you to fuck me,'" he demanded, his molten-gold eyes drifting over my body, his gaze halting on my mouth before resting on my pussy. Seeming unable to make up which part of me he wanted most, his eyes darted back up to my mouth and almost immediately flicked backed down to my sex.

"Fuck me, Ares Darken."

"I'll fuck you until you're hoarse."

Suddenly I recalled how he'd bailed at the last minute. If he did the same to me while I was in such a volatile state, I didn't know what would happen to us.

His knee urged my legs open wider, but I bent a knee, my foot on his hard stomach, ready to kick him off. He gave me a questioning look, lust an unforgiving dark storm in his eyes.

He wouldn't be able to control himself this time. He would have to fuck me, but I still warned, "If you stop in the heat of the moment again, Darken, you'll never have me again. I swear on my future grave."

He cupped my mouth to stop me from finishing the vow. "I forbid you swearing on your life. But I won't stop. You'd have to kill me to make me stop."

I might just do that if he frustrated me again.

"But—" I swallowed the rest.

Caen had warned him this morning that once he slept with any other woman instead of his witch he'd lose her forever, and a kingdom and super-race offspring would be lost to him.

But it would be idiocy to bring up the First Witch right now and screw up my final and possibly only chance of knowing a man intimately. I pushed the witch out of my mind and prayed that Ares wouldn't think of her at this crucial moment.

I needed to tempt him beyond measure and get his cock inside me. The empty ache between my thighs demanded he fill me with his rapid thrusts. If he didn't fuck me good and hard today, I would go crazy. I would do anything to get that one relief, and then that was it.

"Not buts," he said. "It's just you and me now."

So he agreed. The mating frenzy had been merciless toward him as well, and he'd finally answered its call instead of resisting. We would just mate this once, get it out of our system, and move on. He could go back to his witch in a saner state.

I flattened my knee and opened my legs wide for him.

He stared at my pussy with dark fascination before he hovered above me, aiming his hardness at my entrance.

My sex was so wet and hot.

"Now, Ares," I said. "I need you now."

He chuckled. "My lustful Freyja. I'll give you what you want."

His shaft glided into my aching channel. My passage was narrow, yet it accommodated his girth. My walls felt every inch of his hardness, which only heightened my arousal.

Slowly, smoothly, and torturously, he slid in one inch, then another, taking a great care with me. It was a sharp contrast to when he had thrust into me with an explosive strength and slammed to the hilt with one stroke in that alley.

I wanted the same.

Yet he was still taking time moving in another inch as he trembled above me from restraining himself from going any faster.

I lost patience. I was fearful he would back out. I propelled my hips up to help him speed up the action, but he pushed my belly down and pinned me there.

"Slow down," he said. "You're a virgin. I need to be gentle with you." At my dark look, he added, "I realized it was your first time when I saw your blood on me after we had unfinished intercourse in that alley. I won't cause you pain again."

I might have wanted to go slow under other circumstances, but while I had just been torched from inside out by the cursed fire, I wanted his wild passion to make me forget the horror.

"I was no longer a virgin after you thrust so hard in me last time," I said, and he looked so guilty and sorrowful, which wasn't what I intended for him to feel now. "I want a hard fuck, Ares. I've always wanted that. I'm not paper. I'm a wolf girl, the toughest on Earth. Can you match up to me? Show me the storm, if you have it."

His eyes brightened to pure golden at the challenge. "You asked for it, woman."

Ares started pounding hard between my thighs. Faster and faster. He fucked me as he was supposed to—he'd caged his lust for too long. No force on Earth could drag him away from me this time.

I wrapped my legs around his waist to get him to penetrate me freely and deeply.

Each thrust from him, shallow or deep, was bliss.

His cock hit my depth over and over, as if he naturally understood my secret cravings and tempos. I bucked up my hips to fiercely meet his every plunge to speed up my own orgasm, to brace for the release I urgently needed.

In the back of my mind, I was still afraid of being put out, though I knew Ares wouldn't do that to me again. Better safe than sorry. So I fucked him back as hard as I could. The prince raised his head at one point and stared down at me, stunned at my vehemence and strength.

I was a Nephilim, but he didn't know that. I wondered if those women he'd been with had fucked him like I did. The very thought only brought me rage and jealousy.

"How could you?" he murmured in amazement. "You're like my equal. I've never fucked like this." He plunged down, no longer holding back his enhanced hybrid strength.

Our mating became wilder.

He gazed at me, enjoying my reaction as he fucked me.

At some point, I could tell that my face twisted in ecstasy, which only turned him on more. Flesh slapped against flesh. The whole world faded away and mattered no more, except for our mingled, labored breathing and the erotic sounds we produced.

I moaned shamelessly, feeling the coming of my climax. I would get there any second, even if Ares changed his mind now. I, Freyja, the First Witch, would take initiative and wouldn't rely on anyone else to make me come.

Ares seemed to read my thoughts. "I won't leave you, Freyja." His thrusts became lightning fast; his male instinct sensed my need and was desperate to sate me. He pulled out right to the tip, and just as I wanted to mourn at the emptiness, he drove in long and hard. His large, hard cock filled every inch inside me.

He pounded me relentlessly.

The pleasure was shattering me. Melting me. Humbling me.

"Yes, Ares, just like that!" I breathed. "Fuck me just like that!"

A fiery song burst in my veins. A ray of light blossomed alive, streaming between us.

The mating bond had formed.

Ares' eyes glowed pure gold. The bond had chained him as well.

"It can't be," he whispered.

I knew what he meant. The First Witch was his destined mate. Only she could share that bond with him, but he didn't know that the one writhing beneath him in mindless pleasure was the witch.

Would he regret our mating? Would he hate me for cheating him out of his future?

Too late for him now.

He didn't slow his thrusts. His next drive pushed me to the peaks of the waves.

I wanted to roar in victory, but I didn't want anyone to hear that and charge in, despite Ventus guarding the tent.

I wouldn't give the guardians a chance to poke fun at me. Deep inside, I was shy.

My inner walls clenched on Ares' cock. It grew even harder and larger at the stimulation. A deep rumble rose from his chest. Ares gazed at me with such intense possessiveness that I thought he almost mistook me as his witch.

"You're mine," he declared.

Whatever you say.

It wasn't a commitment, and I didn't want his commitment.

But I grinned at him. It was a fabulous fuck. I had finally gotten it out of my system.

My orgasm was long, solid, and damn good, and Ares thrust through it, riding with me and sending me to new highs.

Because of my great satisfaction, I was suddenly in a benevolent mood and started feeling sorry for Ares. I should consider his benefit as well. I didn't want him to lose a great kingdom for this. He still had a chance.

"Ares," I said with a positive smile. "I'm good now. Feel free to stop at any time. You haven't come yet. So, technically, if you stop it right now, you still have a chance with your witch."

He glared at me. "Like hell I'll stop, woman!"

I didn't think he could. His eyes were fiery gold with lava-hot lust.

He pounded between my thighs with explosive vigor.

Every thrust turned into fire again and reignited me.

With a powerful, deep thrust, he pumped his hot seed into my womb with beastly, lustful groans and repressed roars—for the benefit of our audience in the camp.

His climax was long and solid.

"I've never had this much seed before," he said as he gave up one last shudder on top of me. "Soon, I'll take you to a place where I can fuck you without inhibition, and I'll roar the mountains down."

Unless he crossed his witch out of the picture, the day might never come.

But as pleasure lit my every cell, I looked forward to that day we could fuck without inhibition.

~

I lay my head on Ares' broad shoulder, my red hair spilling on his hard chest, just as I'd pictured. I dozed off with contentment, until he woke me up with his hand on my breast.

"You lied to me again, Freyja," he said.

I blinked, trying to return to the world. "Which lie?"

"How many do you have?" he grated. "How many elaborated lies have you woven?"

I tilted my head back to leer at him, still not willing to leave his arms. "I don't know," I said carelessly. "I don't weave elaborated lies."

"The First Witch never headed south," he said, staring hard at me and watching me closely to catch more lies. "But you wanted to go to the Twilight Realm to get the cure, so you pointed the wrong direction and drag us along with you."

"I didn't drag you along. You followed me. More precisely, you forced me."

"Another outrageous lie."

The prince always figured things out a step later, but it wasn't my fault. It wasn't the first time I'd lied to him. He'd have to get over it and move on, instead of looking pissed.

"If you kill me now, you'll just end my suffering earlier," I said. "I have nothing to lose. As for you, you'll have to go back to consult your Oracle again."

"Who said I was going to kill you?"

"You looked like it."

"You don't know anything about my look," he said darkly. "You led us across the continents chasing the ghost, just so you can get the cure. Why did you lie about such an important matter?"

"Like I had a choice?" I said. "I'll be useless to you if I'm too sickly or die on the road. In order to find the witch for you, I need to get the cure first."

"I didn't mean looking for the witch was that important. I meant your curse. You should have told tell me right from the beginning, so we wouldn't have wasted so much time. We could have flown straight to the Fey realm."

"But all you want is your witch."

"And you thought I'd let you die for that?"

He would, wouldn't he? She was everything he could dream of.

Our fucking had changed nothing. It meant nothing. And I was everything but delusional.

He sighed. "Have you ever trusted anyone? Do you even know how?"

"I don't think 'must trust people' is part of my job description," I said.

"We're changing the plan. We're going to Mysth to get you the cure."

"I propose we part our ways from here," I said. "I'll go for it myself. You and your men can turn around and go north to find the witch."

"I won't let you out of my sight," he growled.

"What about your witch? Don't you want to find her sooner?"

"She can wait."

A week ago, he wouldn't have let her wait. He'd been searching for her in great desperation.

"I don't want you to waste time on me," I said.

He sneered. "Still plan to run away from me?" There was deep hurt and anger in his eyes.

"Where can I run? There's only one place I can go and you know where now."

"I won't abandon you, Freyja. You're my responsibility and I'll always keep you safe. But for your lack of faith in me, you'll suffer a consequence."

"What consequence?" I asked.

Heat rose in his molten-gold eyes again.

My pulse spiked. *Oh, damn.*

He flipped me over and had me on all fours.

I'd heard that Dragonian males always preferred to fuck their females from behind.

"As a punishment," he said hoarsely, raw lust laced in his voice. "You'll do whatever I want."

He lifted my ass, his hand coming around to fondle my breast before moving down to brush my pussy.

A hot, hard steel rod was at my entrance, ready to invade my private domain.

I moaned heartily as his large, hard length drove inside me.

I guess I could live with that punishment.

We fucked for hours. I no longer needed to worry that he would leave me wanting. I would enjoy the maximum joyride while it lasted.

I, Freyja, the First Witch, lived only for the moment.

"I never expected this," he said in awe. "It's like you're made for me." He pumped his hot seed inside me just as Mettalum roared in the air before he could roar in pleasure.

Suddenly, all the guardians bellowed in fury.

"Your Highness," Ventus shouted outside our tent. "We've got company!"

CHAPTER 10

The ThunderSong

Ares pulled out of me with a string of profane curses.

I hurried to pick up my other set of travel clothing since my other attire had burned when my skin raged with the cursed fire.

"You stay here. Find cover," Ares ordered, as he swiftly hauled on his sculpted armor.

Like hell I would.

"I'll come back for you, Freyja," he said. "Don't run away from me. I can get you to Mysth faster than anyone can." He grabbed me and kissed me on the mouth. It was a quick, hard kiss, yet pleasure and thrill still buzzed on my skin.

With Ares, this would never get old.

The prince charged out of the tent with his weapons.

I put on my gloves and ran out after him.

Ares mounted Ventus. His men had all been on the guardians' backs, battle ready. Ignis and Glacies hadn't completely recovered, but war wouldn't wait.

Ventus stretched his wings and soared after his brethren.

Wait, Ventus! I called as I flew up, twisted in the air, and landed on the guardian's tail.

Nice jump, Witchling, Ventus said.

Ares turned to me with a snarl. "What are you doing, Freyja?"

"Going to war with you, Your Highness," I said as I moved toward the seat. "Am I not your soldier, as you said?"

"Can't you follow a simple order?" he yelled, his eyes burning darkly. "Why must you defy me at every turn while all I want is to keep you safe?"

"You think the ground is safer with no one defending me?"

"My enemies will focus on me!"

"Your half-brother Keegan heard of the Oracle as well. He's after me, too. He won't stop until you're dead and I'm his."

Rage flashed in Ares' eyes. "He'll never have you."

"You're where it's safer for me," I said. "Have you thought that they can snatch me easily while you're in the air?"

Not that easy, but I wouldn't contradict myself.

"Stay behind me," Ares ordered. "You'll be my shadow and you'll always take shelter behind me. Understand?"

Like hell I would.

I saluted. "Yes, Commander-in-line."

He twisted his torso, reached to grab me, afraid I would fall off, and settled me behind him.

Ventus sped up and joined the rest of the guardians soaring toward the looming battleship that had the name *Insurgent* on its lion-like head.

The ship had a view window, a thick, round body, and a flat tail. Its wings were like a bat's, only larger, thicker, and hostile.

If I had never seen the images of the Angels' advanced, refined battleships in the memories of the dead Angels, I would be fascinated with this rudimentary flying machine.

But it wasn't a toy. It aimed to maim, to kill, and to destroy. It had fought the Angels during the war, and it was the only Earth battleship that hadn't been destroyed by the High Prince of All Angels.

A large Dragonian with blue horns stood by the view window, staring at us with a victorious sneer on his cruel lips. I immediately recognized him through the Dragonian whom I'd killed in the woods. This was Ares' pure-blood half-brother Keegan.

He was the one who had sent the mercenary army to kill the heir and capture me. After I'd talked Ares out of heading to the safe house, the bounty hunters had failed to track us. So Keegan had come in person to finish Ares off. If he succeeded, he would force me to take him to the First Witch. He would abuse me and rape me in the process, as he'd done to so many other women.

Luckily, he didn't know anything about my death touch, and I'd be glad to let him enjoy a full taste of it.

Flanking him on either side were two other mean-looking Dragonian warriors. They carried full sets of angelic weapons.

The guardians were in a battle mode. Glacies moved toward the rear of the battleship. Mettalum took the position at the ship's side, ready to bite into its hull. Ventus swirled up to face the view window at Ares' order.

Ignis was beside us, a stream of fire trampling out of his mouth and spurting onto the window. But his fire had no effect on the glass—it was probably made of special angelic material that could resist earthling weapons.

"Hello, *brother.*" Keegan's sinister voice came out of this ship, which made me want to claw at my skin.

Ares stared back at his half-brother through the window. I

couldn't see his expression, but I felt his cold, murderous rage.

"So, this is it?" Ares asked, his voice devoid of any emotion. "You came to take my life, so you can take my crown, Keegan?"

"A half-blood like you shouldn't be allowed to inherit the throne," Keegan said. "But I'll make a deal with you today. I'll let you live if you hand over the wolf girl."

"The asshole's lying," I shouted from behind Ares.

Keegan wouldn't let the heir live even if Ares gave me up. The pure-blood prince wanted to play first. He wanted to take me in front of his brother and humiliate Ares before he killed him.

"Why do you want her?" Ares asked.

"You know I like firecracker females," Keegan said. "I bet the wolf girl has the beast heat in her and I want to savor it. I'm a male of insatiable appetite, and she might be the first female who can satisfy me. My cock gets hard just by looking at her."

"What makes you think I'll hand you what's mine?" Ares asked.

"Because I might let you live!" Keegan yelled.

"Cunt, take this!" Ares spat as he tossed a spear at the view window.

At the same time, he and his men shot energy beams toward the *Insurgent*.

The ship opened fire.

The guardians wheeled aside speedily, ducking the enemy's fire, while their riders kept firing at the ship.

Fortunately for us, the Earth battleship hadn't developed the Angels' space technology. Though the engineering race had stolen some data from the Angels, they couldn't truly perceive and absorb the advanced alien science.

Though *Insurgent* didn't have high energy weapon at its disposal, it was still lethal as it shot out a barrage of bullets.

Earth weapons couldn't kill me, but those angelblades-turned-bullets would.

In pure panic, I threw up my hands.

To my surprise, a force field erupted out of me and shielded Ventus, Ares, and me, but I wasn't sure if it was effective.

Some form of my magic came only when my life was in absolute mortal danger.

At the same time, a gold shield appeared in Ares' hand and he raised it to block the bullets. But those Angel-killing bullets bounced back before reaching his shield, which meant that my force field had held.

The guardians' riders kept firing beams at the enemy ship,

but those laser beams only sparkled off its thick hull.

Insurgent had the shield technology.

With deafening roars, the four guardians tore into the battleship as one, despite the bullets piercing their scales.

An intense beam of light shot down from the high sky, locking on *Insurgent.*

Insurgent powered down at once.

A larger, silvery spaceship materialized above us. It was an Angel ship—the famous *ThunderSong*—that had helped defeat the Dark Lord of All Angels. It was the High Prince Seth's ship.

The intense beam turned and twisted *Insurgent.*

In front of my eyes, the pure-blood prince's battleship disintegrated from the middle and plunged toward the ground in shreds of fireballs.

The Angel High Prince forbade earthlings from possessing any flying machine, in order to make sure the immortal Fey stayed superior to any other races on Earth. When it came to protect his Fey mate, he was borderline paranoid and unreasonable.

His ship had just destroyed the last, secret Earth battleship.

The guardians were fast enough to retreat to avoid the burned shekels flying in all directions. They were ready to charge the *ThunderSong*. However, they wouldn't stand a chance. None of us would.

ThunderSong was one of the Angels' finest battle spaceships.

The mighty spaceship lowered altitude.

A large Angel with massive black wings stood at the view screen, black-inked tattoos of ancient runes twined from his temple all the way down to his neck. Evidently, he was a high-ranking Archangel.

Standing beside him as his equal was an exotic mortal beauty, who could make any man's blood race too fast, yet none would dare make a move on her. But the formidable Angel wrapped his thick, muscled arm around her slim waist possessively.

Icy light radiated on her almost transparent pale skin and darkness rippled around her. My heart skipped a beat. I'd just met another powerful witch from another planet. She wore three pieces: breastplates and leather shorts and high boots. No females on Earth dressed like that, not even a warrior.

The pair regarded us and the guardians, as if pondering if they should vanquish the flying alligators first. They'd just annihilate a battleship and hadn't blinked. Mercy wasn't their strong suits.

My heart drummed. My throat tightened.

Ares shoved the gold shield toward me and ordered, "Cover yourself!" and raised his ray gun.

I pushed his shield back and stood up on the seat.

"Freyja!" Ares said. "What did I say about being my shadow? Now's not the time to attract attention. Stay down!"

"Now's the perfect time," I said, moving like a flash and cutting in before him.

I stood on Ventus' head.

"No," Ares called, also standing up and trying to get me behind him.

"Do not interfere if you want to get out of this," I hissed.

I pushed my commanding voice into the *ThunderSong,* yet I had no clue if it would work.

"You shall not harm us," I called in ancient angelic tongue. "I have safe passage with Empress Rose. I have her imprint."

I pulled back my left sleeves and showed the mark gifted by the Fey Empress—a red rose with thorns on an angelblade. My mother had passed the symbol of a life debt owed by the Empress on to me at my birth.

The symbol beamed on my wrist.

The Archangel stared at my mark and nodded as the witch said something to him. Then she flicked her wrist.

A force hit me, sucking me into its vortex. I threw my

hand to fend it off, but I was too late.

Before I could finish a panicked thought, I stumbled before the pair in the bridge of the *ThunderSong*. I stabilized myself and sent a glare at the witch, then at the Archangel.

The witch from the other world regarded me as a cat studied a mouse with her piercing grey eyes. Only I wasn't one.

"What is this?" I demanded.

She ignored me but addressed the Archangel. "Gabriel," she purred, breathing out frosty air. "Look, here's another witch."

"A wicked one?" Gabriel asked, looking at me, then returned his gaze to his witch, as if she was his whole world.

Would Ares ever look at me like that for even a second?

The witch laughed darkly. "There's only one wickedest witch, darling."

"Of course, Fia," Gabriel said, brushing a kiss on her rose red lips. "But promise me you won't get into a power match with Empress Rose. She's Seth's mate, and Seth and I are like brothers."

"Then you'll have fun choosing either your mate or your brother," she said.

A wicked witch indeed.

But I didn't blame her. I approved. Didn't all women want

our men to choose us above all? I wondered what the wicked witch would do in my shoes if she knew her man coveted another. Given her nature, I believed that she would knee Ares in the nuts a thousand times over.

I was too nice.

"Fia, be reasonable," Gabriel said. "Aren't I enough for you that you must stir up trouble every other day?"

"Fine, darling," the wicked witch said. "For you, I'll make peace with Rose—and thorn."

The Archangel kissed her in gratitude. She really had him wrapped around her icy fingers. I'd have loved to learn a trick or two on how to tame your formidable mate if I had more time.

The witch kissed the Archangel back with great passion.

"Hey," I called impatiently. "Get a room. But first, why am I here? You have no right—"

The witch broke their heated lips-locking.

"The Dark Lord wants her power as well," she said.

My heart skipped a beat. "How did you know?" I asked. "And what do you know?"

"Of course I know," Fia said, turning to me. "I'm the greatest and wickedest witch. I know all things in the universe."

Her Archangel smiled at her. I sighed. He could see no

fault in her. Even if she stabbed a dagger into his heart, he would still enjoy the wicked sight of her.

Why couldn't I have that kind of power over Ares?

Thinking of Ares, I peeked outside the view screen to see what he was up to and if he was worried about me. But he was gone, as were his men and all the guardians.

Cold bastard! Tears of rage nearly rose to my eyes. How convenient that he'd just abandoned me as fast as he could to preserve himself!

"Embrace your darkness, Witchling," Fia said in disapproval. "Our kind never fears our great, terrible powers." She flicked a finger, and a silver bracelet clutched on my wrist.

Strange runes etched on the bracelet.

"What is it?" I hissed, trying to pull it off. "I don't want it!"

"Oh, you do," she said. "Either I kill you or you wear it, so the old creep can't snatch you away easily. I can't allow him to have your power, which will make it more difficult for me to ice him. But today I'm in a benevolent mood because of my loving mate, so instead of killing you myself to prevent him from getting his hands on you, I'm giving you a fighting chance. But before I leave Earth, you'll have to return the borrowed gift, or I'll hunt you down to the end of the end."

Her Archangel nodded in approval, eating up his mate's crap.

I swallowed a sarcastic comment since it wouldn't be wise to make an enemy out of them. And despite her wickedness, I actually felt kinship toward her.

"You know the Dark Lord's coming?" I asked.

"We've been hunting him," Gabriel said. "He covets my mate's unparalleled TimePortal magic. He'll never lay a finger on her. I'll kill him!"

The Archangel pulled the witch tightly into his arms and they locked lips again.

I rolled my eyes, and at the same time I was full of jealousy of what they had.

Ares had never showed me such tender affection. He was reserving his epic love for his First Witch. Hadn't he just deserted me?

I was done with him, too. It would be like this sooner or later. I should focus on what was best for myself. I would ask the witch and her Archangel to transport me to Mysth when they finished making out. They could get me to the Twilight Realm in a blink.

The wicked witch left her mate's lips and turned her piercing gaze on me. "That's not how it works. You'll have to fight this war so the wheel can turn in our favor. Understand this: there is no shortcut to the ascension of the great power. And yes, we'll get a room soon. This is the second time you said it in your head."

What? How did she get through my mental shield?

Then the scene outside the view screen changed.

The guardians surged, dove, and swooped in the air with all sorts of crazy moves, as if they were looking for the lost treasure in great desperation.

Ares wielded his ray gun and shouted frenetically like a mad man, his eyes wild and bloodshot. Then he saw me in the ship's bridge through the view screen. Rage, relief, and joy churned on his hard face.

He trained his energy weapon toward the *ThunderSong*, but I knew he wouldn't fire at it while I was inside. My heart also leapt in joy at the sight of him. He hadn't left me.

The wicked witch studied Ares in curiosity, and a jab of jealousy crept up in me. I didn't want her staring at him. I didn't want any female to look at him. I was surprised at my sudden territorial ferocity.

I snarled at the wicked witch.

She giggled. "How fun it is to watch your Dragonian go crazy."

Ventus surged toward the *ThunderSong*. In an instant,

Ares was face to face with us outside the screen.

The wicked witch snapped fingers and something in the ship switched on. It might be the sound device since I heard Ares shout his demand, "Return her to me! Right now!"

"Or what?" Fia turned to her Archangel. "These earthlings tire me. Maybe we'll just take the witchling with us. I have a feeling that she can be fun."

Gabriel sighed. "Fia, we talked about this."

"Return me to him or take me to Mysth," I said.

The witch rolled her eyes. "Now you start demanding, too, little one?"

"Little one?" I said outrageously. "You're my age!"

She gave me her wicked laughter. "Never challenge me again, little witch of Earth."

"Try me—" I said, but I didn't even get to finish that at her dismissive wave of a hand.

A blink, and I stood with Ares on Ventus.

Ares steadied me and pulled me right into his arms in a bone-crashing embrace, and *ThunderSong* vanished in a flash.

We settled back in our seats with me sitting on his lap as the guardians headed back to our camp.

"I can't . . . breathe," I said. "Your arms are too tight."

Ares loosened his grip only a little. "You were gone," he

said, his voice shaky, his nostrils flaring. "They took you from me. Next time when I meet them I'll kill them!"

Merlin had said that Ares would always be fiercely protective of me. He couldn't fight his primal instinct to shield his mate. The mating bond had marked me as his. However, Ares didn't have the magical eye, and I doubted if he realized it at all. His mind had been clouded ever since the Oracle had embedded the idea in his head that only the First Witch was his destined mate. To him, I would always be the wolf girl who would lead him to the witch.

"They aren't our enemies," I said, pulling away from him a little to talk sense into him. "They destroyed the *Insurgent* for us."

"They tried to steal you from me!"

I bet he thought everything was his.

"I returned to you, didn't I?" I offered.

He pressed me possessively against his chest again.

"What did they say to you?" he asked.

"They let me borrow a gift," I said, showing him the bracelet.

He frowned at it.

"They took you just to give you a silver bracelet?" This time he drew me back a few inches to peek into my eyes. We really had trust issues with each other despite that we'd had incredible hot sex less than an hour ago.

I shrugged. "They're rich and nice."

I wouldn't tell him about the wicked witch from another world, which would make him think of his own witch.

"They don't look slightly nice to me," he said. "If you like jewelry, you can have every piece in my palace."

This bracelet wasn't for showing off. Fia had warned me of never taking it off.

"Is there anything else you haven't told me about, Freyja?" Ares asked, leaning in, and his intoxicating male scent filled my nostrils and heated my blood.

Ares rubbed his stubble against my face. "What did you hold back this time?"

I knew he would ask about the mark on my wrist eventually.

"I was marked at birth," I said. "With that, I can go to Mysth to ask for the cure."

"Who marked you?"

"My mother," I said. "She died protecting me when the Angels came hunting me."

I immediately regretted of my slip of tongue. I was less guarded with Ares now.

"What about your father?"

"He died after I was conceived."

"Do you know who he was?"

"How could I know? I was only a baby when my mother was gone."

"I'm sorry, Freyja," he said, stroking my hair. "You have me. You have us now."

There were no us when he turned to seek the witch again.

"Why did the Angels hunt you?" he asked. "What do they want from you?"

There we go again.

"I don't know," I said. "I told you they're psychos, monsters."

"You know but you refuse to share the information with me. Eye-patch swore to come for you with the Dark Lord's legion. The Angels won't bring such a formidable army to just hunt some nobody earthling."

Eye-patch also threatened to gut Ares in front of me when he returned, and now I started to fear for Ares' life as much as I feared for mine. Damn the Dragonian prince! He'd brought out all sorts of intense, complicated emotions in me. Life had been simpler before he'd invaded my forest and abducted me.

"You need to let me in so I can best protect you," Ares said. "What can I do to earn your trust, Freyja?"

I swallowed. I'd told him more than I'd told anyone else,

but I couldn't let him know the whole truth. Truth would never set me free. It would cost me everything. If Ares knew I was the only daughter of the Angel King, he would do more than push me away from his warm chest and look at me in disgust.

To distract him, I had to prey on his protective instinct. I brushed my cheek against his chin. "Ares, I'm cold and hungry after this new ordeal," I whined. "I haven't had lunch."

He gazed down at me with a sigh, "I'll go hunting," and wrapped both arms around me to lend me his warrior's body heat.

CHAPTER 11

Mating Call

We left the camp hastily after we had a quick meal. Ares wanted the guardians to fly us straight toward Mysth without taking too many breaks. However, his plan wasn't realistic. Ignis and Glacies hadn't fully recovered from the wounds they had sustained in the fight against the Angels.

When a host of snowy mountains were far behind us, we flew across the war zone. The humans and centaurs had halted fire temporarily. They couldn't spot us at the height we were flying at.

Ares didn't talk much, though his arm was around my waist. He hadn't mentioned a word about his witch. Actually, he'd been trying to avoid the topic, but I knew she was still between us, constantly between us.

Whenever Caen looked at me, his eyes were full of

enmity, and I offered him a sharp smile each time. I needed to watch out for that one, he was the type who would stab me in the back.

After we passed the war zone, Ares' expression darkened. He hadn't had this kind of gloomy mood before we'd fucked. He was probably regretting screwing me. He must have thought that one act on lust had cost him a kingdom, but I couldn't tell him everything the Oracle had told him was lies.

I *was* the First Witch. But how could I bring him the greatest kingdom on Earth when I couldn't even save myself from my curse and my grandfather's legion?

I couldn't bear to see the bitterness on his face if he finally found out that I was the First Witch. He'd pictured how majestic she was. He'd even prayed she was the opposite of me.

Even if he accepted me for who I was, I wasn't a fool to believe we would share a future. He was the Dragonian prince and heir, and I'd never been groomed to be royalty. I would never fit into his complicated, political life.

I was an uncivilized wolf girl in everyone's eyes, or the witch everyone would come to hunt if they knew about my other heritage.

But if he thought I would settle for being his concubine, he was seriously mistaken.

Freyja, Ventus called in my head and jerked me out of my brooding.

What? I asked.

So this is it? he asked.

This is what?

My brothers and I are going to close the bet.

What bet, exactly?

You and the prince get together and he knows who you really are in the end.

We're not together.

You slept with him.

Like that means anything? Seriously? How many woman has he slept with? I bet even you've lost count. I'm just one of the faces in the crowd.

And now I'd become one of the women he bedded and would soon discard after he met his witch. However, he'd already met her but didn't know she was me. And he'd already fucked me—the witch.

This sounded like a total fuck-up.

"Freyja," Ares called me after his long silence.

"What?"

"What are you thinking?"

"Nothing."

"You never think nothing. You little head is always

plotting. What are you scheming now?"

"Tell me, Prince," I asked. "Is it easy to command the pure-blood Dragonians? Can they truly accept you?"

"They'll have to," Ares said, studying me to detect which direction I'd mislead him to. He demanded I trust him, yet he couldn't set an example himself.

It took two to dance.

"My race can't further evolve because of our genetic limitations," he said. "I'm their future. As a hybrid, I'm faster, stronger, and brighter. And when the witch finally joins me—"

He stopped. Seemed like I wasn't the only one who spoke too much.

I hadn't expected that comment to hurt so much, as if he'd stabbed me right in my heart with an angelblade. And I was shocked by my reaction. I'd known from the beginning he would always want her more than me and I'd told myself it wouldn't bother me.

She was his future, and I was his few nights of entertainment.

"I didn't mean—" he said, then stopped himself again.

Of course he meant what he said.

"I don't give a damn," I said. "All we had were a few quick fucks to blow off steam. They meant nothing."

He growled.

"When you have your witch and we part our ways," I added, "we won't even remember each other. I'll forget you just as quickly as you forget me."

A guttural, threatening sound rumbled from his chest.

I ignored my bleeding heart and kept my voice even and carefree. "So, Prince," I asked, "why did Commander North Darken only make you the heir eighteen years ago? Why not earlier?"

"He made me the heir after he had no better candidates. Is that what you meant?"

"I meant no offense," I said.

It seemed our words always got twisted, but now, after we had slept together, they seemed to have more power to hurt each other.

Ares sighed. "It's common knowledge that my father coveted the Fey Empress ever since he'd first laid eyes upon her. She was a princess back then and her emperor father sold her to the Angel King. She sought my father out for an alliance to take down the Angels. My father believed that she would finally choose him. He wanted their offspring to be the heir, but the Fey Empress mated with the High Prince of All Angels. When my father saw all hope of interbreeding with the Fey had faded, he married my mother, a tribal princess of the advanced humans, and I turned from a bastard to the legitimate heir overnight."

"Why didn't your father choose any of your brothers? Don't the Dragonians prefer a pure-blood prince to be their next king?" I asked. "Why give the future throne to a hybrid?"

"My father is a visionary and a revolutionist. He and his scientists collected and studied the genetic makeup of all species and found the advanced humans' genes were superior to any other mortals' on Earth. He believed that the humans were Earth's future. As you can see, with how fast humans breed and evolve. He mated with my mother to guarantee the superiority gene in me, in his offspring."

Commander North Darken also used the lab to enhance his heir's DNA, so Ares was more than any mixed advanced humans and Dragonians. Save Fey, Ares was probably the most advanced specimen on Earth.

"My father hopes I'll rule both humans and Dragonians when he passes," Ares added.

And they believed that with the First Witch joining the hybrid prince, their ambition would be reality. Only they hadn't expected me, the wolf girl, to come along.

Which men could turn away from such a dream and a promise? My anger and bitterness toward Ares ebbed.

"Merlin said humans would take over Earth," I said. "The Fey would fade away."

"The immortals live in a different realm than us," Ares said. "Their magic is only strong in the Twilight Realm. There's no magic on the mortal land."

The world had shifted, as the druid had said.

"Magic is coming to the mortal land," I said.

I was the First Witch and Merlin the First Druid. If I could manage to have offspring, they would inherit my magic and spread it. That was what Merlin had meant that I was the beginning.

I'd never thought that would be possible before, but since Ares could touch me, he could sire my children. I brushed at that thought, and in response, lust swirled alive in me again and clung to me like vines. Warmth pooled between my thighs and my mound was slick with need.

Though his clouded mind couldn't perceive our mating bound, his primal instinct could sense it. Ares tightened his grip on me.

His huge erection pricked against my bottom, and his arm voluntarily moved up until his hand was on my swollen breast.

The mating call grew louder, brighter.

Even though I was on the guardian's back, all I wanted to

go on all fours and raise my rear for him to fuck me from behind. Or I could stay where I was and just haul off my pants and get his cock inside me.

I blinked, shaking my mind out of its lust-filled stupor.

Damn the mating instinct! I thought one fuck would get it out of my system, but the mating frenzy had just started.

I turned to glance at Ares.

He also looked like he wanted to mount me right there, right then, in the high air.

Our reasons were weakening.

His body trembled at his restraint.

We'd made a mistake mating in the tent. How were we going to resist the frenzied call of lust and passion? Even the rapid, chilly current slamming into our faces couldn't cool the heat in our blood.

"How close are we to the shifters' territory, Ventus?" Ares asked through his clenched teeth.

He wanted to land.

I held a hope that we could find a secluded place and fuck again. Maybe next time we could get it out of our system.

"Two more miles, Your Highness," said Ventus.

Ares grunted, but he knew it would be cruel to push the wounded guardians to fly faster.

With the mating fire scorching us, the two miles felt like

two hundred acres.

CHAPTER 12

The Healer

Ares' hands groped at my breasts, his every touch stoking lustful fire higher and higher in me. Until I couldn't bear it.

My mound grew slicker with burning need. I was going to explode if he didn't get his cock inside me within the next second. But there was no chance of that happening for the next hour. This kind of torment was unlike any other.

A majestic castle loomed beneath.

An assembly of armed warriors gathered in the courtyard, looking up at us on alert. Ares unwillingly abandoned his exploration of my body. I didn't protest, though my body wasn't thrilled—despite the crowd below, its carnal need remained urgent.

"Who are they?" I asked, failing to expel the heat from my voice.

"They're Lucas' people," Ares said, endeavoring to gather himself together.

"Are they all shifters?"

"Most of them are," Ares said. "A few of them are hybrids like me. They're my allies. The biggest, scary-looking warrior among them is Ulmar, the pack Alpha."

"Ventus looks scarier than him," I said.

"Thank you for calling me a nightmare," Ventus snapped.

"I'm the girl riding the nightmare. I'm in league with you," I said, twisting my torso to see where Lucas was just as Ignis dove toward the ground.

Lucas would want to talk to his people first.

The Alpha waved at the air. That was his permission for us to land inside the castle.

Ares leapt off the guardian's back and landed gracefully before Ventus touched down.

Don't you want to show off in front of the new people as well, Freyja? Ventus asked.

Nay. I said. *I like people underestimating me.*

So you can trick them and strike them harder?

Not harder, but fatally, I said.

Lucas was talking to his Alpha intensely, and the other warriors surrounded them.

Ares strode toward them in his confident, powerful gaits.

Einarr and the other three Dragonians flanked him, and no one laid their hands on their weapons.

I was left behind. I slowly climbed off Ventus and groomed the beast while watching the shifters from the corner of my eyes.

The shifter stopped asking Lucas questions and turned to Ares. A few of them glanced in my direction, found nothing too impressive, and no longer paid us any mind. They must have seen the flying alligators before, so they didn't look alarmed.

As for me, I had my cloak covering half my face. I was shorter and more slender than any of the warriors and seemingly posed no threat to them. The only odd thing about me was I wore gloves, but the shifters didn't know why, so they didn't care much.

Ulmer and Ares crossed their forearms in greeting.

"I have terrible news from Atlantis, Prince Darken," Ulmer said.

I pricked my ears to listen.

Ares remained cool. "What is it, Alpha Ulmer? I left home four months ago."

After being ambushed by the mercenary army hired by his half-brother, the prince and his men had discarded their communication devices, thanks to my brilliant, free counsel.

"My informants reported back two days ago that Commander North Darken is on his death bed," Ulmer said. "A power bid has started in Atlantis. The word on the street is that your pure-breed brothers are taking control of the capital. Your generals have sent words to every post across the continents to ask you to return to Atlantis at once."

I turned toward them.

Ares looked across the space and met my gaze, his face sullen, his eyes dark. He would need to return to Atlantis, so here was where we would say goodbye. My heart clenched at this turn of events. I hadn't expected to part with him so soon. I might never see him again.

"Let's go to my quarters, Prince," said Ulmer. "We need to talk alone."

Ares tore his gaze from me. The alpha and the prince treaded toward the main stone stairs that led up to the Alpha's quarters in the castle.

A few shifters came around to arrange accommodation for the guardians and us.

Lucas headed straight toward me. "Come with me, Freyja."

"Where to?" I asked.

"Don't you trust me?" he asked with a smile.

Why did everyone want me to trust them? I never asked

them to trust me.

I looked at Ares' retreating figure. He didn't even bother to glance back.

"Fine," I told Lucas. "Lead the way."

I kept my hood over my face and my gloves on my hands, and I kept a safe distance between us as he walked me toward the gate.

"You don't need to be so careful with me, Freyja," Lucas said.

"Don't you know better?" I said. "You know my curse."

"That's why I'm taking you to see the healer," he said. "She lives in the woods outside the castle."

"No healer can help me except the Fey Empress," I said.

"Galena is a gifted one," Lucas said. "If she can help you, you don't need to go to the Twilight Realm. You can live among us. And your wolves will be welcome here."

This was a large shifter community. They'd welcome my pack. But I wouldn't choose to live here, no matter how friendly Lucas was. I didn't want to be bound by their rules.

My wolves and I were wild and free.

"Galena can't touch me either," I said.

"She'll have a way," Lucas said. "Don't worry, Freyja. Give her a chance."

If she knew I was the curse of the Earth, she'd worry, but I didn't want to discourage Lucas.

We left the castle behind us. It didn't take me long to spy the woods of marigold and lime ahead, which made me miss my forest and my pack achingly. Our home looked like waves of tea rose from afar in the golden sunlight. At night, the wind was wicked fun.

If Galena could heal me, then anyone could touch me. Ares wouldn't have exclusive rights over my body. Lucas could touch me then. He had even invited me to live here.

"Lucas," I said, "you know Ares and I—"

"It doesn't matter," he said. "It's circumstantial. When he isn't the only one who can touch you, you'll have more choices. You can live the life you want. I want you to have that chance. And," he paused, "the prince will eventually pick the—"

"—First Witch," I finished it for him. "I don't give a fuck."

I could almost hear the tear of my heart, even though I'd known that Ares would always choose the witch over me. Our mating hadn't changed a thing in that regard.

I stared at the ground, fighting back tears. After Ares had walked away with the shifter Alpha without sparing me a glance, I already felt like I was being dumped. I didn't believe I had fallen for him, but I wasn't an unfeeling being either.

"No one touched me for nearly twenty-two years," I said. "Whoever I touched ended up dead."

"You don't need to explain," Lucas said, holding my gloved hands.

"Lucas," I called in alarm.

He grinned. "This won't kill me."

I didn't toss his hand away. I didn't want to hurt his feelings, but eventually, I would hurt him. I already felt sorrow at that.

"Even if Galena can't heal you, Freyja, I'll go with you to the end of the Earth for the cure."

I smiled at him. "I hope we don't need to go to the end of the Earth."

He squeezed my gloved hand gently.

With Lucas, everything was easy. There wasn't this stomach-turning thrill ride or gut-wrenching upset, but peace and warmth for a change. In the end, wasn't that all we looked for?

Passion would fade, but loyalty and friendship stayed.

We held hands and crossed an old bridge over a silvery stream. Ahead was a wooden cabin built inside a vast tree. That had to be where the healer abided.

A blur charged from the side, and I tensed. The Angel

instinct in me immediately sensed a threat. I yanked my hand out of Lucas, stepped away from him, and pulled off my gloves.

"It's fine, Freyja," Lucas said, glancing at my bare hands then at a brown bear that came into view. "No one will harm you while I'm here." He stepped between me and the shifter in a bear form.

The bear growled. From her attitude, I believed she considered Lucas hers.

I moved and stood beside Lucas. I needed no one to shield me. And I was no one's shadow.

The animal bared her fangs, glaring at me with her dark brown eyes.

"I've seen much bigger fangs," I told her.

It snarled, wanting very much to pin me down and maul me. As if I would let that happen!

Come near me, teddy bear, and see how you like playing with me.

My hands were ready. The First Witch never backed off from a fight. Well, I did run when the fight involved Angels.

The shifter didn't register my threat. I realized I could push into an animal's mind, but not a shifter's. They had a natural mental block, and I wasn't as trained as Merlin.

"Amber, stop it!" Lucas said. "You won't treat my friend

that way."

The bear blocked the other end of the bridge. She wouldn't allow me to pass.

But I never, ever, asked for permission to cross a bridge.

"Get out of my way," Lucas commanded, his muscles bulged, ready to shift and fight her. "I'm taking Freyja to see Galena."

A blink, and in the next instant, a brown-haired, naked woman stood in the bear's place. She looked a couple of years younger than me. She was pretty and had a nice body, but Lucas didn't seem to be affected. I figured shifters saw naked bodies all the time, however, I recalled the heat in Lucas' eyes when he'd first seen me nude at the lake.

Amber put her hands on her broad hips. "Galena won't see the cursed," she said with a vengeful grin. "You should know what you associate with, Lucas."

I felt the blood drain from my face. How could a shifter healer know? What did she know? Should I return at night to shut her up for good?

"Don't you ever badmouth my friend," Lucas snarled. "I want to hear the words from Galena herself."

Amber raised her chin to study me, the hostility in her eyes growing stronger. Shifters didn't like other species anyway. "Galena might not know what exactly this one is, but she had a dream last night warning her of this redhead. Your friend is the black death. She drains life force from all living things. She'll destroy the old Earth that we inhabit."

A dream, a warning, and a prophecy. Could it get worse?

Who sent the lousy dream to a shifter healer? Could it be the Oracle messing with me again? She didn't want me healed. She didn't want me to stay here.

Lucas retorted in anger, "And now you're the healer's mouthpiece?"

"I became her apprentice after you left me," said Amber.

So they had a history.

"I want to hear what Galena has to say in person," Lucas said. "She'd better not to make an enemy of me."

"She's like a mother to you, Lucas," Amber said. "You would go against her for a stranger? How long have you known this redhead who hides her face?"

"Move!" Lucas bared his teeth. "I won't warn you again."

The muscles enlarged on his shoulders. He was starting to shift.

"Lucas," I said, "I don't want to meet the healer anymore."

"But Freyja!" he said.

"She can do nothing for me," I said. "Let's get out of here. Please."

I turned and headed back to the other end of the bridge. I didn't see Amber carrying a weapon, but I stayed alert.

The stream rushed beneath my feet.

Lucas caught up with me in two long strides. I was certain he'd had a glaring match with his old girlfriend.

"I'm sorry, Freyja," he said.

"There's nothing to be sorry for," I said. "You've been kind to me from the beginning."

"Do you want to go back to the castle right away?" he asked. "If not, I want to show you my haunt as a boy."

"Then it must be a naughty place," I said.

Lucas laughed. "Come and see."

I pulled on my gloves and followed him.

Near the end of the woods, Lucas grabbed my gloved hand and made me sprint with him.

"When I say jump, you have to jump," he said.

"I'm not going to jump just because you say so," I said.

"Either way, you'll jump forward or down," he said.

Down didn't seem like a good option.

I saw a vast rift looming toward us at our speed. Instinctively, I leapt over it with Lucas. "What the hell is that?" I laughed when I landed a few feet from the rift.

Lucas grinned. "I haven't met a girl who can run so fast and jump so far. Not even our shifters."

If he knew I was half Angel, he wouldn't smirk then.

I treaded back to see the rift.

Over twenty feet below was the bluest, clearest water I'd ever seen. Cave rocks gathered the natural pool in its embrace and purple plants grew along the rocky walls.

"I know you love to bathe," Lucas said.

"But not today," I said.

If I wasn't in such a frustrating mood, I'd dive in.

Lately, ever since I'd gone on this unfortunate journey with Ares, I'd been either extremely high or low, as if all of a sudden I'd developed a personality disorder. I also noticed now that I was so used to be around Ares, my energy level dropped a great deal with his absence.

Lucas looked disappointed. He'd put in an effort to make me feel better and I wasn't enjoying it.

"It's so beautiful and peaceful here," I said. "Can we sit down and just watch the shining water?" I didn't want to think of Ares, and I wanted to get away from the world outside, even for a few minutes.

"Of course we can," said Lucas, cheerful now.

We settled down on a rock at the edge of the hollow, our feet dangling down, Lucas' hand on my shoulder. It was a light caress, unlike Ares', whose touch could bruise me.

I stared down at the water that seemed to freeze in time,

yet my mind kept returning to Ares.

I shouldn't have slept with him. The mating bond had enslaved me. No matter where I went, there was no escape from the thoughts, the scent, and the scorching touch of him.

Sound of flapping wings approached, and a shadow fell over my face.

My heart pounded fiercely before I realized they weren't Angel wings, but a guardian's.

Ares roared from Ventus' back. "Hands off, Shifter, if you want them attached!"

How had he found us so soon? Wasn't he in the middle of an all-important meeting?

I jumped to my feet and moved a few yards away from the rift, so I wouldn't fall into the deep pond by mishap or Ares' design. I put my hands on my hips in defiance and suddenly felt I was coming alive.

"What are you doing here, Ares?" I demanded, as if I owned this land.

"Trying to catch you!" he said, landing.

I narrowed my eyes. "Catch me for what? I'm not a fish."

"It'll be easier if you're a dumb fish I can pack in a bottle," he said. "I thought you went missing again."

"You knew I went with Lucas," I said. "Everyone saw us leaving the castle together. They had to tell you. There's no need for you to come chase me like this."

Ares' darkened eyes burned with jealous rage. "So you two can fool around?"

Lucas stood beside me. "We aren't fooling around. I wanted Freyja to see the healer for the curse."

Ventus stood by, eyeing me disapprovingly, yet watched with a zealous interest.

"Where is this *healer* you spoke of? Why do I not see them?" Ares asked, his eyes still spitting fire.

"She can't heal me, so I didn't waste my time on her," I said with a shrug, not wanting to explain further.

"So you came here to hold hands with the shifter?" Ares asked. "To sneak around behind my back?"

"Freyja doesn't belong to you, Ares," Lucas said. "You've chosen another woman. It's not fair to Freyja that you'll cast her aside when you meet your mate."

"Is that your excuse to steal her from me?" With a roar, Ares lunged at Lucas. "No one steals her from me!"

I slid between them, and Ares halted just in time. "Move," he shouted at me. There was no sanity or kindness in his eyes.

"Freyja, step aside," Lucas also urged.

"Now you're defending the shifter?" Ares asked. "Don't you know he can't handle you? No one else can, except for me. Don't forget I'm the only man who can touch you."

All the pent-up emotions in me exploded. Ares wanted to lay a claim on me, but he still wanted his witch. Just as Lucas had said, Ares would dump me at the first chance when the witch popped out.

"Fuck you, Darken. Fuck you!" I shouted.

"You did that already, multiple times!" he barked back. "And every time you couldn't get enough of me. You were all over me. Have you already forgotten?"

"You won't get another!" I said.

"I don't want another." he said. "You think I want more of you after suffering through your arrogance? No woman dares to treat me this way. No one has dared disrespect me."

"Luckily I'm not your woman and I'll never be one of them," I said.

He sneered. "Where will you find another man to touch you?"

"You won't be the only one who can touch me when I get rid of this curse," I said. "But you'll be the only one who will never get to touch me again."

He roared like thunder and pulled me aside.

In a blur, Ares and Lucas charged each other, throwing punches. They fell to the ground, a tangle of limbs as they wrestled, kicked, and pounded their opponent.

"Stop!" I screamed, but they wouldn't listen. Wouldn't stop.

More wings flapped overhead and I looked up to see the rest of the guardians had arrived with their riders.

This was no longer a private event.

The men watched with grim expressions. No one dared to interfere when their prince was in a jealous rage.

Ares would beat Lucas to death because he thought he was executing a punishment. But I knew he would regret it for the rest of his life if he killed Lucas.

Lucas was about to shift to better battle Ares, and Ares would bury a knife in his gut.

I lunged toward Ares to get him off Lucas, and he shoved me back without looking. I flew back at the force. Before I knew it, I fell into the rift with a loud splash and a louder yelp.

"Freyja!" I heard both Ares and Lucas calling my name.

Ares jumped after me. With one stroke, he swam to my side and grabbed me to him. "Are you hurt, Freyja? Did I hurt you?"

I struggled to break free, but he wouldn't let me go, showing his iron strength.

I beat his chest rapidly with my fists, and he let me vent.

And then I was sobbing, and dropping my head on his

shoulder.

"Shush," he said, an arm sliding around me while he paddled in the water to keep us afloat. "You're fine now. I'm here, and I'm sorry."

Was it the first time he'd ever apologized?

"I don't want this," I said.

"What do you want, Freyja?" he asked, his voice uncharacteristically gentle. "Whatever you want, I'll give it to you."

"I don't know what I want."

"I panicked when I got out of the meeting and didn't see you." He started to kiss the tears off on my face. Agony and longing and desire in his eyes only reflected mine. "I didn't know what came over me. I'd never lost control like this. You constantly drive me mad."

I parted my lips and stared at him.

The mating frenzy was doing this to us both with punishing force. My advantage was that I had the knowledge but he didn't. He was all wrapped up in the Oracle's prophecy. But I wasn't going to share the truth, despite his pain and devastation. Even with knowing, I wasn't in any better shape than he was.

Our bond demanded us to mate at every chance we got, so we could reproduce. As we rebelled and shoved it aside, not ready to commit to each other even after we'd mated, it pushed right back at us with bruising blows.

It inflicted us with crazed rage when we weren't together.

I clasped my hands behind his neck. Now with our skin pressed together, the rage receded, but the need to mate started pounding in my blood stream. Lust was bright and dark in Ares' eyes as well.

"I need to keep you safe, Freyja," he said. "You can't just wander off like that. What did I say about being my shadow? Did you even pay attention to anything I said?"

"You said it for your own convenience. When you went to the meeting with the shifter Alpha, you didn't even spare me a glance."

He paused for a second. "Is that why it irked you? Then you should just tell me straight instead of leaving the castle. What if something had happened to you? What if the Angels had snatched you while I wasn't around? You need to learn discipline instead of constantly striking out ruthlessly. We're not in Atlantis, surrounded by my great army. I don't even have enough guards to protect you here."

The light from above shone on his face. My breath caught in my throat. The Dragonian prince was indeed magnificent, and it wasn't just my lust talking.

Though he could take my breath away every time I set my

eyes upon him, I wasn't thrilled at his lecture. And I suddenly remembered the terrible news the Alpha had delivered.

"Why do I need your guards to protect me?" I said. "I did well all by myself before you came along. The Angels wouldn't have found me if you hadn't exposed me."

Guilt dampened his eyes, and I thought of exploiting it.

"I also saved you," he argued. This one wouldn't stay down for long. "I'm the best man to protect you. When we get to Atlantis—"

"There's no Atlantis for me," I said. "You'll go with your men. I'm heading to Mysth alone." I needed to get to Mysth before my grandfather's goons came to Earth and before my cursed fire and ice struck again. "You can kill me if you want," I continued, "but I'm not going to your city or finding your witch before I get my cure. I'm living on a borrowed time. Death at your hands would be mercy."

I was actually thankful he had to return to Atlantis. I didn't want him to have any conflict with the Fey and get himself killed by my uncle. I had safe passage to the Fey realm, but he and his men didn't.

"I won't kill you," he said. "But you'll go wherever I go."

I unclasped my hands behind his neck to shove him away from me, but his grip on me only tightened. "Some women might let you treat them as your plaything," I spat. "But you'll regret it deeply if you think you can treat me the same."

"When did I ever treat you as a plaything?" he said. "You're the one who considers me your boy toy. You think you can use me like that and then dump me without any consequence? I won't allow such treatment! From day one, you've been trying to leave me. Is this your new scheme to discard me? You won't succeed, Freyja."

The Dragonian heir was born with the skill to twist words.

His large hand rest on my nape and pulled me a little further so he could stare into my eyes with a determined, furious look.

"Let me go," I said, "and you'll have your witch in the end."

"But I don't have her, thanks to you pointing the opposite direction."

It was still about his witch. He would only leave me alone once he had her. He wanted to make sure he would be the one to throw me away instead of allowing me to walk away in dignity.

"If you drag me to Atlantis," I said, "I won't be useful to you. The curse of fire and ice can hit me at anytime. I might not survive it next time. You can't be so heartless—"

"That's why I'm taking you to Mysth first," he said.

My mouth opened, yet no words flowed out.

"But—" I finally managed to find my voice. Had I heard it wrong? He wouldn't put me first.

"Tell me that's not your plan, Your Highness!" Caen called from above.

I looked up—every man and beast was watching us from around the ring of the rift. I hadn't noticed that we had an audience all this time. I'd been completely absorbed in Ares. Despite my rage and hurt, it had felt so good to be in his arms.

My face flamed in embarrassment.

"We'll escort Freyja to the Fey territory," Ares said clearly.

"But your father is on his death bed, Prince!" Caen said.

"I've served the Commander well and long. My father has other sons. They'll fulfill their duties to him. He'll have to do without me this time. I grieve for that, but Freyja can't wait."

"You'd choose a girl you've known for a couple of weeks over your own father?" Caen said incredulously.

"The cursed fire may come back anytime and hurt her," Ares said. "The Angels are still hunting her. She needs me more than anyone."

"We can split into two teams," said Caen. "I'll return with

you to Atlantis, and the rest of the crew can escort her to the Fey realm."

"No," Ares said, "I won't let her out of my sight for a second."

"What?" I said, not liking this turn. "I'm not your property, Prince Darken. It'll work best for everyone if we just split from here. I know how to get to Mysth by myself, and I don't want you to lose a crown, your father, or anything, for my sake."

He ignored me, as if I hadn't spoken, and focused on his cousin.

"Do you hear what you're saying, Prince?" Caen shouted. "What's gotten into you? It's not like you've never had a woman before. In fact, you've had more women than any Dragonian has ever had, but you never lost your mind over any of them. You've never allowed any woman to decide your course except your future mate, to whom you should be heading to, after attend to your father. Ares, you need to wake up from this madness!"

"I'm more awake than ever," Ares said. "I've never been so sure in my life as in this moment what really matters to me. You'll return to Atlantis to take care of things on my behalf. Ignis will fly you back."

Ignis grunted. He didn't want to go back to Atlantis alone.

But an order was an order. A ring of fire puffed out of his mouth and hit the water a few feet from us.

"Ignis, careful!" Ares called. "Freyja's here!"

"What about your fated mate—the First Witch?" Caen asked bitterly. "Do you have a new plan for her as well?"

"To hell with the witch," Ares said.

Everyone was shocked into silence, as was I.

He couldn't really mean it. A Dragonian never strayed from a decided path.

"Please, Your Highness," Caen begged as he realized his prince was going to be a lost cause. "Don't throw away your soon-to-be inherited kingdom for a night of passion. This isn't you. When you find your destined mate, you'll know this girl is nothing compared to the powerful First Witch. We've come so far for your future queen. A future queen who will bring you the greatest kingdom on Earth."

"Say no more, Caen," Ares snapped. "My decision is final, and you'll leave at first light tomorrow."

"Ares—" I said, but he slanted his mouth on mine and shut me up.

"I feel like crying," Ventus called from above. "Someone give me a handkerchief."

Crocodile tears?

Some small rocks and chunks of dirt flew down at the

guardian's emotional push as he kept staring down at us with his large, blue eyes.

"Ventus," I broke the kiss and called, "I don't want my hair to get dirty."

The guardian shook his huge head. "Can't believe a wolf girl can be so spoiled." He was citing Ares' words. "But never mind me. Are you two going to stay in the water forever? Your skin will get all wrinkled and you'll look like an old woman."

"We probably should get out," Ares said, his lips grazing over the shell of my ear, "unless you want me to help you with your bath. In that case, I'm more than happy—"

"I don't want your help," I said. "I'm tired."

"Ventus!" Ares called.

The guardian wheeled his rear toward us. As I wondered if he meant to insult us, he swept his tail down the cave.

Ares lifted me up effortlessly and put me on Ventus' tail before he grabbed its end. With a thunderous chuckle, Ventus sailed into the air with us dangled on its mighty scales.

CHAPTER 13

New High

We stayed in the castle for the night. I shared the luxury guest suite with Ares. Though I grew up with wolves, I always had a penchant for lavishness. Maybe it was the corrupted Angel blood in my veins. I was the Angel King's bastard daughter after all.

I strode toward the master bedroom, not shy from claiming it for my own. Ares looked at me from across the room with dark longing on his face. He was waiting for me to invite him to my bed. With a snicker, I booted the door shut in his face.

I could bear a grudge for a long time.

Our afternoon's quarrel still rang in my ear. He'd insulted and humiliated me in public. I'd sworn at him, and he'd barked back that he had no interest in fucking me again. And then he'd mocked at my misery that I couldn't find another man to touch me.

I'd declared he would be the only one who would never get to touch me again.

I was keeping my word now.

The more we mated, the more complicated it got. Nothing good would come out of dallying with a Dragonian prince. What would happen when I couldn't live without him and he didn't want me anymore?

The mating call buzzed in my veins, but I fought back, denying it and myself.

I wouldn't be with a man who would choose another woman over me because of his ambition.

I kicked off my boots and threw myself on the bed. It was vast and soft. It could accommodate both Ares and me. I could lay my head on his broad chest after we fucked. I sighed. I could bury nose in his body; I liked his scent.

Stop it!

Fire filled my veins and ice filled my heart.

~

We left the next day at dawn.

Lucas stayed with us, despite his fight with Ares. I learned that they were childhood friends. All of Ares' team members were like Ares' brothers, but one of them was a traitor.

Even after Ares had thrown out the horned Dragonian, *Insurgent* had still found us. So Tyrone might not be the leak. Who else could it be? I'd excluded Lucas and Einarr. There was no motivation for them. However, loads of Dragonians didn't like the idea of having a half-blood leading them. The mole had to be Boomer, Jericko, or Caen. I'd be watching.

Now that Ares and I had bonded, though not to his knowledge, I'd have to consider his benefits if they didn't collide with mine.

The morning air was fresh and crisp in the high sky. A palette of colors rose and spread across the horizon, bracing for the rise of the sun.

The world hadn't awoken beneath us. It felt as if we were the only ones who walked the Earth and flew the sky. It made me happy that I was sharing this with Ares.

He sensed my mood and tucked me against his chest. His warmth and solidness and confidence made me want to purr, until I remembered I was still holding a grudge against him. I stayed in his arms for a few more seconds before I pried his hand off my waist.

He sighed, but didn't sneak his arm around me again.

Ventus sped up, and the chilly current rushed past my face.

"Do you want to sit behind me so I can shield the wind from you?" Ares asked. "Since we've already shared the height of intimacy, you don't need to feel shy to cling to me."

"I'm not shy, and I'm fine as I am now," I said in a clipped tone, determined to keep my distance.

To show my steel will to push further, I inched to the edge of the seat. My body protested for moving further away from Ares. It had no pride and no shame. It only had carnal need. Every second of the day, it wanted Ares to fuck it. A lot of times when I battled it, its need won.

I tried to turn my attention to the road.

We flew across a range of mountains, rivers, and cities after cities, and in between were the wrecks of the civilization tumbled down by war. The world was constantly shifting and remolding. Prosperous cities were leveled, and from the ruin rose a new civilization that would soon become old. In the end, a rainstorm of time would wash away every hint of their existence.

Would Ares and I still be around to see how the new world replaced the old?

He had thousands of years to go. And I might be immortal, as Eye-patch had revealed. I felt no joy at having eternity. I would have to watch my own world and those I cared for fade away and never return.

I would be all alone.

At the glimpse of the future, I wanted to edge back to Ares and bury my face on his warm chest as my body craved, as my instinct called.

Why did I keep resisting him?

Because Ares wanted me only for sex. Especially when the mating frenzy drove him as hard as it pushed me. Yet in his higher mind, he put his witch there.

Weren't a few quick bangs all I'd wanted as well? Then why was I so irked? He would keep fucking me until he got his witch, if I let him. He wasn't even as eager as before to find her, but that could only mean he wanted to fuck me longer before he had a new, shinier toy.

What a calculating bastard.

Ares leaned toward me, using his velvet, seductive voice on me. His mating need was calling to him. I stretched forward, almost prone on Ventus' scales, to get out of the prince's reach.

I listened keenly to Ventus, as if every nonsense word the flying alligator puffed out was gold.

You completely misread him, Witchling, Ventus started.

Do I? I sneered.

I see. You're still jealous of the witch. But you're the witch. Why are you jealous of yourself? I haven't heard crazier things than that.

You don't understand, Ventus.

A Dragonian, especially the very best of them, said the guardian, *never goes astray from a decided path, but he's doing that for you. He no longer pursues the witch with single-minded determination because of you. And you only try to find all sorts of excuses to fight your feelings for him. It won't end well. Don't say I didn't warn you.*

"What are you two whispering about?" Ares demanded, his gruff voice cutting through the mental communication between the guardian and me. "I won't tolerate conspiracy. If there's anything you two have to say, you say it out loud."

He really hated being excluded, didn't he?

"Freyja and I were discussing relationships," Ventus said.

I bristled. "We were not."

"What's to discuss?" Ares said. "You don't discuss it. You do it."

With that, he had his hands on my waist, lifted me up, and pulled me to his lap. "Stop fighting me," he said, his voice husky and rich, and heat blazed in my belly and all the way down, until liquid fire pooled between my thighs.

I shivered with lust.

"We need to come to an agreement," Ares said, "so we can both have some peace. I've had enough of this."

"Enough of what?" Ventus asked. He wanted more soap opera.

"Stay out of this, Ventus," Ares said. "You've been encouraging her all along. Don't think I'm deaf, even though I can't hear you two whispering dark schemes. In the future when Freyja doesn't behave, I'll hold you responsible as well."

Ventus swept his tail sheepishly at his master's scolding. He thought he could always watch others burn and laugh on the sideline unscathed.

I chuckled at his humiliation, and he puffed.

"We'll stop at my Moonshade Villa," Ares said.

"It's a bit detour, if you don't mind me saying that, Your Highness," Ventus said.

"It's only half a day's flight," Ares said. "I need to go there and set things straight with Freyja."

"You can set whatever straight with me here," I said. Ventus might back me up here.

"Not here," Ares said, tugging me closer to him. He wanted no space between us.

"Is Moonshade a safe house?" I asked.

"It's my private resort," Ares said. "Only Ventus knows its location. We won't be ambushed, if that's your concern."

"We need to get to Mysth as soon as possible. I don't

want the cursed fire breaking out on the road. It'll burn Ventus!"

"Ventus is tough," Ares said.

"I'm not!" Ventus cried.

"Didn't I melt your ice and cool your fire, Freyja?" Ares coaxed.

"We got lucky," I said, unable to quench the fear in my voice. "What if you can't help me the next time?"

"In order to stop the curse from striking again," Ares said, "I need to calm you first. That's why we need to go to the Moonshade. We'll get to the Fey realm in a few days."

"What are you going to do to calm me?" I challenged.

"Oh, you know," he said, his hand moving up and cupping my breast.

My lips parted, but I stifled a moan of pleasure.

I'd rejected him last night, though I had been tormented by the unfulfilled lust through the night as well. I'd showed him the new-leaf Freyja wasn't weak and carnal. I'd promised him that he wouldn't get a piece of my ass again. I had to stick to my honor, and I did have it.

Yet thrill buzzed in my blood at what was coming. My nipples grew taut.

"I'm gonna take a nap," I murmured.

Didn't get any sleep last night, Witchling? Venus

snickered. He was one who held a grudge as well. *The prince didn't either. I can tell just by how irritable he's now.*

I ignored him and dozed off, only to be awoken by a shout of my name.

I flashed open my eyes and found my face pressing on Ares' chest, my hands seizing his massive, armored arm.

He gazed down at me with amused tenderness.

I looked around wildly. My heartbeat resumed to normal when I didn't spot Angels.

A vast rainforest loomed ahead. Endless shades of orange, red, and blue waved beneath us in the wind.

"I heard shouts," I said.

"We're at the Moonshade," Ares said. "Ignis wants to say goodbye. That's why he yelled your name."

I snapped my head to look for the guardian of fire and saw he was already by Ventus' side.

May we meet again, Witchling, Ignis said, his fiery eyes gazing at me. *I'll miss out on a lot of excitement.*

I blinked. *Why? Where are you going?*

"Returning to Atlantis," Ignis said.

It flooded back to me that Ares had assigned Ignis to return Caen to the capital to handle the royal business while his father lay on his death bed.

"Must you go, Ignis?" I asked. "Isn't it wasting resources?

Why can't your Dragonian passenger find a horse?" I ignored Caen's glare and added, "There're plenty of transportation on the ground. By gathering his wits and spending some money, he'll get a fast one."

He won't agree, Ignis sighed.

From his sad, hopeful eyes, I knew he wished Caen would be man enough to prove him wrong and release him, but the selfish, hard-ass royal cousin only nodded to Ares and nudged Ignis to fly toward the rainforest.

I turned to Ares, wanting to beg him to let Ignis accompany us. I hadn't expected to grow so attached to the guardians. It hurt to see even one of them leave. But looking at Ares, I knew his decision was final. The Dragonian prince was everything but sentimental.

Ignis gently bumped his snout on my side, his version of a hug, and shot toward the endless trees, a stream of fire in his wake.

Ventus abruptly dropped altitude and flew between the forest and cliffs half covered by the clouds. It was a stunning sight, but I was more concerned that other guardians weren't following us.

"What—" I asked, then my jaw dropped at a vast natural cave in the midriff of the cliff. At this height, clouds flowed by it.

"Are you ready, Freyja?" Ares asked.

"Ready for what?"

Ventus thrust his head toward the mouth of the cave. Ares held me against his chest, grabbed a vine rope hanging from the top of the cave, and flung forward.

I yelped when I realized my feet dangled in the empty air.

"I've got you." Ares looked down at me with a mischievous smirk. "You like jumping, don't you?"

"Who said I liked jumping?" I hissed.

"No matter," he said. "We jump."

"Wait!"

He let go of the vine and landed with my legs wrapping around his waist and my arms coiling around his neck.

"I'll never let you fall," he said. "Have some faith in me, my darling Freyja."

I hissed at him again, but I didn't release him. My body liked clinging to his.

"Ventus, pick us up in the morning," Ares shouted toward the cave's mouth.

"I'm not a cavewoman," I said. "Why must we—"

Then I saw we were inside a modern villa—the Moonshade.

CHAPTER 14

Moonshade Villa

I unhooked myself from Ares and surveyed a vast lodge with modern facilities. My gaze fell on an oversized bed with a marble headboard in the center. Realization dawned on me—the bed was custom-made to accommodate an Angel's wings.

My heart pounded and my breath shortened. Ares had just led us into an Angel's lair.

"Why do you look fearful, Freyja?" Ares asked, his thumb and forefinger holding my jaw in place as he studied me. "I thought you would be pleased if I brought you here."

Strong magic slammed into me, thicker than ancient wine and brighter than the sunlight spilled in. There was no menace in it.

The High Prince of All Angels had once abided here. The imprint of his power lingered even after he'd abandoned this place decades ago.

It wasn't just magic sparking around me; lust was dense in the air. The Angel Prince had brought his fey mate here for their first mating. They'd never returned after that.

"Have no fear, Freyja," Ares said. "You're safe here with me. I claimed this place for my own a decade ago. I set a trap at the entrance and only I can come and go safely. And now you."

He didn't know the history of the haunt. If I told him about it, I would ruin the mood. Second, he would start to interrogate me.

The Dragonian prince had no magic bones in him and couldn't see the power trace— perhaps Ares was immune to all magic. However, he had to feel the lust in the air. Desire was heavy in his molten-gold eyes.

He gazed down at me. "We're finally alone."

"Why did you bring me here?" I asked, trying to dilute the heated yearning in my voice.

"You know why," he said and scooped me into his arms and strode toward the bed, his rapid heartbeat echoing with mine.

He'd promised that he'd fuck me without inhibition, and what place was better for that purpose than this secluded villa?

My body was giddy, yet my mind remained undecided.

Instead of placing me in bed with care, Ares tossed me to it, for the fun of it. I rolled to the other end, and he was in it the next second.

Without a word, his large hand got into my clothes and cupped my breast. Before I could protest, he flattened me, his mouth slanting on mine.

When his wicked tongue thrust through my open lips with commanding force and stroked my hard palate, my eyes rolled back at the pleasure. His hand caressed my nipple roughly, just the way I liked.

He stripped me of my clothes, and in a flash he was half nude.

His golden-brown torso rippled with muscles and pressed on mine, his chest crushed against my breasts. He deepened his kiss, his tongue mating with mine with urgent need.

A moan of pleasure escaped me.

I bucked my hips up to show him what I had in mind.

I wanted to see his large, hard cock. I wanted to hold it and stroke it, and when I played with it for a while to my liking, I wanted it in my pussy. I would ride him like there was no tomorrow.

I might not have any tomorrows. I bent a knee, my toes latching on his trousers to drag it down. Ares groaned and broke the kiss. "Not yet," he said roughly, his hand grabbing my ankle to stop me.

"Didn't you bring me here to fuck me?" I asked.

"I want to stick my cock inside your hot, tight pussy more than anything," he said in a ragged, lust-charged voice. "But I want to take it slow. I want to savor you."

"You just want to torture me," I whimpered.

He half chuckled, half choked on his own lust. "That, too. But I'm with you."

Fine, I would let him play. He'd had countless women before, and I was inexperienced. I didn't mind learning a few new tricks.

"At least take your pants off," I breathed. "Let me see your dick."

I was forever fascinated with it.

"You drive a hard bargain, woman," he sighed.

As he dropped his trousers, his impressive cock sprang free, jerking upward proudly.

I let out a gasp.

Ares' eyelids grew more hooded as he watched me stare at his cock with unbridled lust. His hand slid down to the hot place between my thighs and explored it.

His fingers caressed my clit in tortuously slow circles.

I lifted my bare pussy to press tighter against his hand,

signaling him to enter me.

He obliged me and brushed open my folds. I could feel my inner walls clenching around his powerful finger. It glided in and out, its stroking quickening.

I moaned, and he twirled his finger inside me, caressing my walls.

I grabbed his hair and gasped, "More, Ares, I want more!"

A few more twirls and twists like that, and I would come hard.

The prince pulled his finger out.

"Ares!" I warned.

He inserted his finger into his mouth and suckled my juice from them. "The best taste ever," he murmured.

"Put your finger back in," I instructed. "And don't pull it out unless I say so."

"I can do that," he said. "But let's talk first."

My eyes went wild. "Are you crazy?"

"I need your full attention."

Fury sizzled in me; aching need rushed in my bloodstream. I was so frustrated that I almost wanted to kick him in the head, but that would do me no good. I had to entice him instead of antagonizing him if I ever wanted him to finish what he'd started and sate me.

"What do you want to talk about?" I hissed.

Lust was a rainstorm raging over his body, yet the Dragonian prince held an impressive self-control.

"Whenever you're in bed with me," he said, "you're hotter than anything. But when you leave the bed, you're cold toward me. Why is that?"

"You're hot and cold to me as well," I said.

"That was before I officially slept with you."

"It changed nothing."

"It's changed everything, Freyja," he said quietly.

Was he going to blame me for ruining his chance with the witch? When he'd rejected me twice before, he'd said that if he broke his celibacy and fucked any woman other than his true mate, he would lose the First Witch and the kingdom she was going to bring along.

"I didn't force you," I said.

"Will you be this defensive forever?" he asked in exasperation. "I brought you here, not just to lay with you. I need to know why you're acting differently lately. You're hostile. I want no more misunderstanding between us. I'm not a fucking mind-reader. I'm a warrior. If you aren't happy, and if there's anything you want, you'll have to tell me directly. We're done playing games. Tell me you understand this. Tell me what you want, and I'll fuck you."

"I want you to fuck me."

"That's not the answer I'm looking for. Tell me what's been bothering you. Help me to understand."

"Other than that, I don't know what I want," I said.

"That's exactly your problem, isn't it?"

A sudden anger rose in me. "Like you have no problems? What am I to you, Ares? Am I your fucking whore?"

He sighed. "Your body and mind tell you a different thing, don't they? Have I ever treated you like a whore?"

"You're using me to warm your bed until you can get the witch to heat it."

Dark amusement sparked in his eyes. "You're jealous."

"Jealous?" I snorted. "I don't do jealousy. If I were, I wouldn't have handed you the noblewoman. If I were jealous, I would have clawed her eyes out when she laid her fingers on you like that." To be honest, I'd almost charged to her when she tried to hook up with Ares.

"You almost succeeded in tricking me," he said, temper rising. "If I hadn't known better, I'd have let you ruin my future. I told you all actions have consequences. I haven't even punished you for that yet."

I swayed my hips, and his breathing grew ragged and his eyes darkened with barely contained lust.

"You can punish me now," I purred, "as hard as you want."

He pressed his hand on my belly, his every touch the fire of pleasure. In the back of my mind, I started to worry as the temperature in my body kept rising. I hated being weak at the knees around Ares, so I'd resisted the mating call yesterday. Now lust was like raging fire in my blood. What if it turned to cursed fire if I didn't get a release soon?

"Be still," Ares said as he struggled to control his own lust. His cock was throbbing. A bead of moisture formed on its crown. He wanted to fuck me just as badly as I wanted to fuck him. "We're not done talking," he grated.

A lusty moan resonated in the room. It hadn't come from me. I snapped my head to the left. The magic imprint of the past swirled alive.

The Fey Empress' image lay beside me on the soft sheet. Her Angel unfurled his massive wings and thrust into her as she spread her legs wide for him. When he pulled out a few inches, I gasped at his manhood. It was as impressive as Ares'.

Had my lust conjured the image? Or was their lust so strong in this villa that my magical eyes caught it all again?

The lust and love between the Fey Empress and her Angel consort had been epic. Because of their love, they'd changed the future of Earth and given earthlings a surviving and evolving space. If they hadn't felt that degree of lust that could shake the Heavens, my father—the Angel King—would still have ruled and enslaved Earth.

What would have become of me if King Agro were alive?

One significant fuck between a man and a woman could change history.

"Ares?" I whispered.

"Why are you distracted, Freyja?" Ares asked. "We need to finish this conversation. It's important."

He had such a hard time controlling his need and desire that he had to blame me for my writhing under his hand. But how could I lie still while I was watching—

The Angel fucked the Fey harder. She gasped and moaned in delight. His cock slid in and out of her pink pussy with rapid speed.

Their mating heated my blood.

"Ares, I can't take it," I whimpered. "Tell me what you want, quickly, and I'll give it all to you."

"I want you, Freyja," his said, his thumb tracing across my quivering lower lip.

I turned my face away from the coupling, opened my mouth, and caught his finger between my teeth. He half shut his eyes as my tongue licked it.

"I've always wanted you," he said. "I've never wanted anyone as much as I want you. I wanted you the moment I laid eyes upon you. Even after you threw a dagger at me, my blood still ran hot for you. I thought you might have put a spell on me back then, but you aren't a witch. After I met the fake one and lost you in that store, I knew what you truly meant to me. And when I saw that fucking Angel thrusting his blade toward you . . . I'd never been so afraid in my life. At that moment, I vowed I would give up anything and anyone, if I could get you back alive."

Though I was flattered that he'd wanted me so much right from the beginning, it was a bad idea to keep talking while the ache between my thighs pulsed with urgent, unbearable need.

The mating heat rendered me mindless and I couldn't register much of his words.

Right beside me, the Angel and the Fey were still at it, moaning and groaning. I turned slightly to glance at them.

The Angel pulled his mate up, placing her legs on his shoulders as he pounded her relentlessly.

"I crossed one continent after another," Ares said, "believing the next best thing would be over the horizon while it was right in front of me."

What was he talking about? He wasn't talking about me, was he?

I gave his cock a heated glance before turning to watch

my phantom neighbors screw each other.

The High Prince slowed down to tease his mate. I could see every detail—how his large cock plunged into her shadowy valley and her folds locked his length. He withdrew an inch and thrust back in before quickening his pace.

I licked my lips. "Do you think the witch is waiting in the horizon, Ares?"

"Are you listening to me?" Ares asked, his voice harsh. "Do you want me to keep pursuing her? Is that what you truly want?"

How could I know with my sex-muddled mind? While he saw only me naked in front of him, I was tormented by the overstimulation. The Angel and the Fey were fucking right in front of my face!

"Huh?" I asked. "You've wanted the witch all along. Now you're going to forget about her and move on?"

"Have you listened to what I told you?" he asked with exasperation. "Why do you keep looking to your left?"

"You aren't exactly the romantic type, Prince Darken." I sighed, trying to focus and get my shit together. "As the future ruler of Atlantis, you're one of the most famous bachelors on Earth. Your reputation precedes you. You've never fallen for a female. You don't pursue relationships. You've always been a heartbreaker. Even when you set out to seek the witch, you didn't want her for her. You want what she'll offer you."

"Have I broken your heart?" he snickered. "I know I broke your maidenhead!"

"Because I didn't give you a chance to break my heart," I hissed, my mind suddenly sharpening due to my anger.

"Why do you think I want to break your heart?" he asked.

I waved at him dismissively. "I misspoke. I'll never fall for you. There's no heart there for you to break or tear."

He looked hurt, which diluted the stormy lust in his eyes.

That wasn't what I'd intended. I'd be foolish to discourage him while my body was aching with lust. I would say whatever I wanted after I had my relief.

The Fey Empress sank her fingers into the Angel's thighs as he slammed into her, burying himself in her to the hilt. Her mouth fell open and she let out a lusty moan of pleasure. He drew back and thrust into her again, each stroke harder, faster, each stroke filled with more passion. Her thighs quivered and her grip on the Angel tightened. I was sure she was about to come.

"I might be what you said," Ares said. "But after I met you, things changed. I've changed."

"A Dragonian never diverts from a set path," I murmured.

"Don't forget I'm a hybrid. I'm half-advanced human, like

you."

"You still wanted to find the witch even after you slept with me."

"Not exactly. I admit I was a bit curious. I wanted to see who she was, but I wasn't going to marry her."

"She's beautiful and powerful beyond measure," I reminded him.

"I don't care. I met you."

"The Oracle said she's your fated mate."

"To hell with the Oracle. To hell with the First Witch."

He grabbed me, his mouth sealing my doubts, and maneuvered me onto his lap. He lifted my ass without breaking our kiss, the head of his cock aimed at my entrance.

The prince bucked up his hips, and his shaft penetrated through my tight channel and seated deeply inside me.

I screamed in pleasure.

"Your pussy is so tight, yet so resilient," he said huskily. "It fits my cock perfectly."

I placed my hands on his massive shoulders, ready for a frenzy ride.

"Is this what you want, Freyja?" he asked, thrusting up.

I moaned. "Yes, Ares, yes!"

"You're getting what you want, female," he promised.

Ares kept his hands on my hips, his pace growing faster

with each thrust. There was no gentleness in his moves. I could take it. I liked it. I'd always wanted it this way. I was a Nephilim, stronger than any mortal, except for the hybrid Dragonian prince.

He was one of a kind, unbreakable and unwavering. His strength rippled in each thrust, sending me over the high waves that tried to reach the dark stars.

"I'm going to fuck you without inhibition," he said. "Can you take it?"

"Bring it on, Prince," I purred.

Ares unleashed his lust, driving deeper and thrusting wildly into me, his movements so fast, they blurred my vision. I tried to move up and down, but he overpowered me. I was amazed that every pounding was more forceful than the previous ones, as if the hybrid prince had endless power.

My body lit up. Then I realized again that Ares was my electricity, and fucking me was the best way to recharge me. I absorbed his energy, yet I didn't drain him like I did others. When the next wave pushed me to the divinely high, I gave him back some of mine.

Ares gasped in awe, feeling my reciprocal energy feed.

My fingers sank into his shoulders as I rocked against him, meeting his frenzied thrust. My bountiful breasts bounced on my chest. While he fucked me hard, I fucked him back harder.

For a while, neither one of us spoke. We screwed each other like two wild beasts. He drove up and I plunged down. Every inch of his shaft rubbed my every spot in just the right way.

"I've never fucked like this," he said. "I've never met my match until you."

The pleasure was undoing me and remolding me, yet I craved more. My Dragonian was able to give me more. He could fuck at such strength and speed endlessly. My moans went out with a few short screams, and Ares bent his head and pulled my nipple into his mouth and suckled hard.

His cock grew larger and harder inside me, and his animalistic, erotic groans set me ablaze all over again.

I was wild. I was free. I was fire and ice, and my Dragonian was the savage who made my blood flow in a rush. But he thought I was savage.

As hard waves hit us both, I could no longer hold back.

I roared as my inner walls convulsed around his cock, milking it violently.

Ares thrust through my climax, and then he roared his own release against my breast. He crashed me against him hard, his generous seed pumping into my womb. I sat still on top of him to enjoy the incredible sensation as my orgasm lingered.

His mouth moved to mine, kissing me with tenderness and gratitude.

Sunlight basked me.

My chest swelled with warmth and pride. For my twenty-one years, I had been death. Ares had rewritten me.

He lifted me up off him, and I resisted.

Ares chuckled. "I need to clean you first." He pulled his hard cock out of me, came back with a towel, and started wiping at my sex. He cleaned himself and tossed the towel across the room.

"I never spilled this much seed with anyone before," he said. "Not even close. I used to think I might be barren."

"You're anything but barren," I said. "You flooded my insides."

He laughed, leaning over and pressing a casual kiss on my lips.

The prince lay beside me, and I rested my head on his shoulder as he wrapped an arm tightly around me. Thankfully, the image of the Angel Prince and his Fey mate was no longer beside me, or I wouldn't be able to lie still next to Ares with a content, stupid grin on my face.

I didn't understand why he wanted to snuggle. I was so energized I wanted him to fuck me again. I would mimic how the Fey Empress and her Angel had done. The magical imprint of their mating was probably for training purposes. When the Angel had claimed the Fey, she was a virgin, though she hadn't acted like one either.

My hand traced circles on Ares' chest, and he liked it, not knowing my actual interest was on his cock. I didn't want to be too obvious. I counted to four before moving my hand down. The ache between my thighs had been sated, but I still wanted his cock inside me.

The mating frenzy was still in effect.

Lust rained in Ares' golden eyes as well.

"I found you, Freyja," he said.

My heart stuttered. He hadn't meant he'd found the witch, had he?

"My instinct tells me you're my mate," he said, "though you aren't the witch."

I swallowed.

"You didn't exactly find me. You abducted me," I reminded him softly.

"It was meant to be," he said in a dismissive tone. The Dragonian prince still didn't like anyone, especially me, disagreeing with him. "It's worked out just fine."

"According to who?" I asked.

"After we acquire the cure for you in Mysth," he said,

stroking my hair, "we'll return to Atlantis. You'll be guarded by an army. I'll make sure no Angel can ever get near you."

I admired his confidence, but when the Dark Lord's legion came, even the High Prince and his Fallen Angel force would suffer great loss. The Dragonian army stood no chance.

Right now, while he chose to escort me to Myth instead of returning to Atlantis to prepare to ascend to the throne, his surviving half-brother was taking the opportunity to grab power.

"It would be safer for me to go to the Twilight Realm alone," I said.

He growled.

"I have safe passage into the Fey realm," I said, "but you don't. Any conflict between you and the Fey, and I can kiss the cure goodbye. Without your flamboyant flying guardians to attract attentions, the Angels won't find me."

That wasn't completely true. My grandfather had turned his sights on me. The blood imprint would make sure his horde could get to me anytime. I was betting on my luck they hadn't reached Earth yet, though my time was running out. I didn't want Ares and his team to go down with me when the Angels army caught up with me.

I didn't want Ares to be sad if there was no cure for me in the Twilight Realm. I wanted him to move on.

He would be the new Commander. He would have a new life. Though arrogant, formidable, and often insufferable, he had a good heart. He would be a good Dragonian King.

"If you think I'll let you out of my sight," Ares snapped, "you're kidding yourself. I know how to handle the Fey. I'll only make sure they give you the cure."

"I swear on my life," I said, "if you follow my plan, I'll come to Atlantis to look you up after I have the cure. And I'll bring the First Witch to you."

"I forbid you from swearing on your life," he grated. "Don't you understand, Freyja? I brought you here not just to have sex with you. I brought you here to claim you."

Why did he want to claim me? To what purpose?

"I don't want the witch," he continued. "I want you. Don't you know my heart beats only for you? Lightning struck me at the first sight of you. I now know why."

"I didn't see lightning strike you when you came to my forest," I insisted. "I saw only the beating wings of the guardians."

"It's a figure of speech," he said in irritation. "My point is, I no longer want to fight what my heart wants."

"Don't you give up too soon, Prince?" I asked. "The Oracle said only the First Witch can be your mate. The witch will not only bring you the strongest nation on Earth; your combined bloodline will produce superior offspring. Isn't that what all Dragonians have dreamt about since the beginning of your race? And with the witch, you'll secure your rule."

He narrowed his eyes. "Did you eavesdrop over my private conversation with my cousin?"

"You two were loud enough for the whole camp to hear."

"We whispered."

"No man will give up a kingdom for a woman, Ares."

"I'll give up my life for you in a heartbeat, so what's a kingdom compared to my life? And what's a kingdom to me when all I'll have is a dead heart inside?"

"You haven't met her yet," I said softly and felt a sudden stab of pain at my own lies. But I needed to persuade him to let me go. Being around me would bring him death. The Angel legion would never cease hunting me.

I would find a way to ditch Ares after today, after I fucked him a few more rounds in this villa. I wanted to kiss every inch of his skin and burn it to my memory at the end of the day. That was all I would have.

But first I needed to prepare him to move on.

"How do you know another woman won't make you feel this way?" I asked. "Look at me, Darken, what could I possibly offer you?"

"Everything," he said. "You've become my existence, though you're also the bane of it. I don't care what my people want anymore. I don't care about their dreams, hopes, and obsessions. I've served them for centuries. Now I go for what I want. And that is you. Honestly, Freyja, the throne is a high place made of chains, thorns, and blades."

"That's your lust talking, Prince."

"It's beyond lust. No one can make me feel the way you do, not even the First Witch. I'm damn sure of that."

"When the gorgeous, powerful First Witch shows up, you'll bash your bloody head against the wall for the wrong choice you're trying to make today."

She—I—wasn't that gorgeous. As for powerful? Hardly.

"They say no one is more beautiful than the Fey Empress," he said. "I thought so until I saw you. But I'm not looking for the beauty of the Earth or the most powerful woman. I've met many of them in my long years, but no one has touched me. Not until you. I know all this time I've been looking for you. Not the witch. That's why the Oracle sent me to find your first."

"But you said before I was the test and trial that you needed to overcome to find the witch."

He frowned. "Must you remember every thoughtless word I said?"

"Then why did you say them?"

"I'm a man! It's what a man does."

I tried to move away from him to show my displeasure at his snappiness, but he had an iron grip on me.

"I'll bring you to my—our—home where you'll be safe," he coaxed, softening his voice, "after we get you the cure."

If Empress Rose didn't kill me, her realm would be the safest for me.

"So everyone will cheer for you getting a new concubine?" I said.

"I don't have a concubine," he said. "Neither will you be one."

I sneered. "I don't even get an official title?"

He turned my face to him, his thumb and forefinger holding my chin firmly, as he peeked into my eyes. "Freyja, you'll be my future queen, my only woman."

What? I stared hard at him, my mouth agape. Earth! He was serious. He was fucking insane!

"You—you want me to be your future queen?"

He arched an eyebrow. "Why the hell not? You're fun and fiercely sexy."

"A queen isn't supposed to be fun," I hissed. "And being fun and sexy should not be listed as the qualities for a good queen."

"Then what's your definition of a good queen?" he asked with genuine curiosity. "I'm all ears."

"I'm not getting into that right now," I said, sensing his trap. "But you know well that I wasn't bred to be a queen. I have no first-hand knowledge how the court works." Though I'd gained and accumulated intel through a few death touches.

"You'll learn the job on the spot," he said, amusement dancing in his eyes.

"You think this is a fucking joke?" I raise my voice in great irritation. "It's your kingdom you're putting on the line, Ares!"

"You can't screw up too badly," he said. "I've been watching you since the first day, Freyja. You have a keen mind. Other than you bearing a grudge for a very long time, you're adaptable. When we settle down in my palace, I'll hire the best tutors for you on court etiquettes, fashion, hostess duties, among others. You love parties and fancy dresses, don't you?" He brushed a quick kiss on my brow to show his support. "I have every confidence in you, my good Freyja."

I snickered. "And Your Majesty will accept my gratitude in the end."

"I will when you say it sweetly," he said. "Do you have any idea how many noblewomen fought nearly to death for the position beside me?"

"They might think it's the best job in the world serving the trifle court at day and you at night." I sent him a sly glance. "But I'm not one of them, and I'm not a noblewoman. I may be young, but I wasn't born yesterday. A gilded cage is still a cage."

Ares scowled at me. His subjects might be trembling at his temper, but I wasn't one of them either, as I'd told him. When he saw that he couldn't intimidate me, he withdrew his touch from my body. It immediately protested at the lack of his caress and demanded I make up to the prince and get his hands on me again. I ignored my shameless body's urges.

"If you don't want to be my future wife," Ares said, pointing at his cock, which had hardened again, "you won't get it either. This comes with the whole package." He went further to remove my head from his shoulder, gritting his teeth as he moved a few inches away from me, and folded his arms across his broad chest.

Very mature.

"I'll have to live with that then," I said regretfully, eyeing his proud, strong cock.

Ares sighed.

"Think of it," he said, resuming his velvet, hypnotic voice on me. "Don't you want to be fucked every night and every morning?"

Was that how he used to seduce females to his bed? I wondered if those noblewomen liked his blunt, crude talk.

"That depends," I said.

"Think how good you'll feel when I stroke your pussy," he said, "as I did a minute ago. I'll thrust my tongue inside, hitting every sweet spot. I'll make you moan."

His eyes became hooded, dangerous lust dancing in them.

I licked my lips at the erotic pictures, my pulse racing. Angels were the most carnal species in the universe, and I got all of their weaknesses.

"Then my cock will replace my tongue," he continued, meeting my glazing eyes. "It'll go in slowly, taking its time before it penetrates deeper. Your hot, tight, lovely pussy is like a flower. It makes my cock so hard. Its petals will open for my cock as my crown pushes through your heated channel. Your pussy wraps around my shaft so tightly and sucks me in. Earth! My cock is aching. I need to fuck you now."

I swallowed, my throat parching with burning lust. The mounds of my glistening sex throbbed in need.

"Picture how good you'll feel," he said, his voice laced with desire, "when my cock drives into your depth and fills every inch of your pussy."

"Ares," I whimpered, swaying my hips.

He followed my movements and his intense eyes stared at my bare sex as I now propelled my crotch toward him.

"Ares," I whined, "please."

"Say yes to my proposal, sweetheart," he said, pumping his hand up and down his thick, hard shaft. "Be my mate, and you can have this as much as you want, any time you want. Don't you want to experience again how I make you come? You come long and hard every time, milking my cock, like no one else could."

"Why don't you demonstrate now to remind me how your cock makes me feel? How it fills my pussy completely?" I said, my eyelids heavy with the burden of desire.

Every muscle on his face displayed his lust, making it unbelievably erotic. I balled my fists and pressed my legs together in case I lost control and jumped on him. Because right now, I was thinking of landing on top of him, forcing his cock inside my pussy, and riding him savagely.

"Say yes," he said. "Just one word and I'll fuck you senseless. I'll go so deep you won't even believe it." His hand gripped the broad, heavy crown of his dick. I wanted to replace his hand with my mouth, but I'd need a better strategy.

He was a master of seduction and an expert on all things

in the bedroom, given how he had fucked me. But I was a quick learner. I could seduce him back.

"Think of it," I said with my sultriest voice. "How will you feel if I have your cock in my mouth?"

He sucked in a sharp breath, his eyes brightening like the stars in the dark sky.

"First, my hot, plump lips will wrap around the head of your cock," I continued, "enjoying its silky feel. My tongue will join the feast and lick your length all the way up before sweeping across the ring of your crown. Your steel rod turns me on like no other. I have to taste the moist bead from your slit."

His eyes rolled to the back of his head. Ares spread his legs wide, his large hand squeezing his cock.

Yet, I had no mercy.

"Then my lips will glide down your shaft," I said. "Slowly at first, one inch, then another inch. I'll lose patience because I want all of your length in my hot mouth. I'll start going faster. My mouth will move up and down, suckling you so hard that you can't take it anymore. Still, my little, pointed tongue will lick your cock all over, and my teeth graze . . ."

A deep groan emitted from his chest and Ares grabbed me.

Before I could react, I found myself pressed against the

full window, trapped by the Dragonian prince as his strong hand wrapped around my waist possessively. His ragged breathing was on my temple, and his silky steel rod pricked against my lower back.

My breath shortened, my heart raced, and my blood buzzed with thrilled anticipation.

His cock spanked my ass hard.

"That's how I spank a naughty girl," he said hoarsely.

I moaned at the rush of desire I felt at his words, the dip in my belly filling with need each time his cock slapped against my ass, and swayed my hips with excitement. After the spanking, I wanted a good, long fuck. I arched my back and pushed my butt back, baring my plump pussy to him.

"You're the fire in my blood," he said, voice slurring with the storm of lust. "I can never get rid of it. So I'd better ride it."

His hand let go of my waist and pinned my wrists above my head. His thumb and finger prodded open my plump folds. With a forceful thrust, he shoved his cock into my pussy from behind. One stroke and it slammed to the hilt.

Its hardness and heaviness filled me; its pressure made me want to come right away.

"Ares," I whispered. "Fuck me like this is our last time."

His hand reached around to fondle my breast before

moving to flick my swollen clit.

"I'll fuck you the way you want, the way I want," he said hoarsely, huskily, "but it won't be our last time. It's only the beginning."

I pushed backwards and started riding his rigid length. Fucking him was spectacular, majestic . . . delicious and addictive.

A guttural sound tore from his chest.

Clouds drifted by beneath our feet. The rainforest across from the cliff shivered in the wind as if it could feel our pleasure.

The side of my face pressed against the cold glass, contrasting with the heat radiating off my body.

Ares thrust into me, every stroke deeper and powerful than the previous. My Dragonian prince's strength was infinite. A lusty moan that wasn't mine sighed beside me. Right in this spot, the Angel High Prince had fucked his mate, exactly how Ares was fucking me now.

Same place, same positions, different lovers. My present entwined with the Fey Empress' past. Was it a merely coincidence?

Though Ares couldn't see the magical imprint of their mating, he could sense my amplified sexual appetite. He gripped my hips and pumped faster and harder. Pleasure slithered up my spine.

"You're made for me, Freyja," he said in approval.

I wasn't going to argue with him when the rhythm of his rapid thrusts mesmerized and enthralled me. The sound of flesh slapping flesh was maddeningly erotic.

"Do you know this lair you claimed," I said between my moans, "once belonged to an Angel?"

"Yeah?" He didn't slow down his thrust.

"It belonged to the High Prince Seth. He and his Fey came here to mate. They left their imprint all over."

"You can see that?" he asked in amazement.

Perhaps I should slip in another truth? Like the fact that I was the First Witch?

He'd chosen me. Shouldn't I try to be brutally honest with him, no matter the consequences?

The thought of the consequences stopped me cold.

There might never be a good time to break the news, my conscience chimed in, but I'd learned not to listen to it. I only listened to my survival instinct.

Ares adapted to the combinations of long thrusts with rapid shorter ones. Each thrust was powerful enough to push me to the brink of insanity. His other hand caressed and rubbed my sensitive peak in circles.

"They fucked right here," I breathed out.

That aroused him more. "Did he fuck her hard as I'm fucking you?" he asked.

His cock penetrated through my inner walls, his thrusting relentless. My body became his instrument.

"It's not a competition," I moaned as pleasure ripped through me.

Ares thrust into my core with brutal strength.

"Yes, Ares!" I screamed.

"My cock will be the only cock for you all your lifetime," he said. "And I'll fuck only you in my lifetime."

The witch was indeed out of the picture.

One hand pressing on the window, one hand gripping his thigh, I panted, "Ares, I'm coming!"

He stilled and pinned me to stop me from moving on his length to reach my climax.

I regretted giving him such a warning. I should have just quietly taken my release instead of announcing it like a victory. Lust burst in my veins, in urgent need of venting out, yet the damned Dragonian prince wouldn't allow me.

I was going to erupt.

"Say your vow of fidelity," he said, "and I'll let you have the longest, hardest orgasm."

As if I have a choice. I couldn't touch any other males, except Merlin, without sending them to death anyway.

"Fine," I said, "I'll have only your cock and no one else's. Now get on with it. Fuck me with all you got."

His next powerful thrust sent me slamming into the window as he pounded between my thighs with abandon. Pleasure exploded in me like spewing lava. This kind of sex wasn't for the faint-hearted.

The glass rattled in the window pane.

I half closed my eyes, at the mercy of the mating instinct.

"The best fuck I've ever had," Ares groaned. "I can fuck you however I want without inhibition. I want to fuck you forever. Never stop." With that, his cock rammed into me again, sending me to a new realm of pleasure.

A blur of short, rapid thrusts—his thick crown rubbing and pushing at the edge of my entrance, until his whole length drove into my depth, pushing the waves in me higher. I cried mercy when the next high tide swept me under and shattering spasms rocked me to the molten core.

My release cascaded through me, and I roared victoriously.

Yet Ares wouldn't give me a break. His cock thrust through my orgasm as if it was king of the realm. I forgot to argue who should dominate the new territory when another wave of orgasm pushed at my shore.

Then, I felt Ares' transformation. He was still thrusting

inside me wildly, yet his form grew large and almost beastly. I'd seen him shift when he had fought the Angels in the alley, but we weren't battling now.

"My mate! My female! My future queen!" he roared, and I felt his lengthening fangs grazing the side of my neck. He bent his head down and sank his teeth into the spot above the curve of my shoulder and neck.

I cried at the sudden burst of pain. Then an indescribable sensation washed over the pain and in that moment I knew pleasure I had never known before. I screamed hoarsely as the heavenly and hellish pleasure opened the floodgate of my orgasms again.

One arm coiled around my waist to keep me with him, one hand ramming onto the window to support his weight and mine at the violent assault of our combined climax, Ares raised his head from my neck and roared in triumph.

His cock thrust in me like never-ceasing fire, and he emptied his warm seed in me.

"I claim you as my mate," he declared.

"Wait!" Was that why he bit me? Was it some kind of claiming ritual?

"It's beautifully done," he said with great satisfaction.

"You can't just claim me like that!" I cried.

"Why not?" he asked. "I've already claimed you with my

cock. Now I've sealed it with my mark on you. Everyone will know you belong to me now, Freyja. You're mine forever. There's no escape, no running away, and no turning back for both of us."

I shouldn't have been so surprised. The Dragonian prince always took what he wanted. He might have never asked anyone for permission his whole life, so he didn't know any other way. With me, he needed to learn the other way.

But my body was so divinely happy from the sequence of orgasms, the latter ones overlapping the previous ones with bigger waves. I couldn't utter any objection for the moment.

Later, I'd give him a piece of my mind.

But then, I'd never felt such peace and contentment. I'd never felt so desired and cherished.

The mating ritual somehow fulfilled the requirements of our mating bond that demanded our absolute commitment to each other.

"Ares," I whispered.

A mystic force swelled inside me, changing me. With that, every barrier in me shattered and the walls toppled down.

"Yes, my sweet Freyja?" Ares answered lazily. His happiness rippled toward me like a sunbeam through our bond. His cock remained rock hard in me and he started to thrust again, tenderly and slowly. He was making love to me.

"The Oracle said I would recognize my mate," he said, "when I joined with her in body, mind, and soul. It was never the witch but you who are my true mate, Freyja. The fucking Oracle lied to me."

It was time to tell him.

Fuck the consequences.

"I, Freyja, *am* the First Witch," I said in the voice of power.

His instinct had sensed that I was his mate when he'd first met me, but the Oracle's promise had shrouded his mind, so he couldn't wrap his head around the fact that I was his witch, right in front of him, while he'd searched so hard for her.

With my magic reaching him and streaming inside him, he was no longer blind. His mark on me cleared all obstacles and there was no doubt in his mind that I was indeed what I claimed to be—the First Witch and his fated mate.

He stared at our lighted mating bond as the mythical, dominating, and beautiful force streamed between us.

His body tensed against me like a snapped whip. His cock only grew harder.

I stilled, too, as the world froze before it exploded.

The window before us shattered with horrible, piercing sound.

With a furious roar, Ares pulled me back with him, faster than a flash across the night sky.

CHAPTER 15

The Legion

The mountains trembled in terror and the forest shuddered, not because of Ares' roars.

Massive wings covered the sky and blotted out the sun.

The horde of the Dark Lord's Angels had arrived.

They swarmed the place.

Outside the window, their black wings swung in the air, their cold, determined gazes on me and Ares.

They'd come to take me to my grandfather, so he could harvest my power, as he'd done to others who had powers he coveted. The magic in me would revive him, and he would break me. It didn't matter that I was his blood. All that mattered to him was his uncontested power and throne in the universe.

I was his means to regain the glory he had lost.

Ares tugged me behind him. "Get dressed, quickly!" he ordered.

I shoved on my clothes hastily. Under the circumstances, there was no need to go nude.

The Angels outside the villa all wore full armor. Eyepatch had told them about my lethal touch, so their skin was all covered. From what I knew, their armors could shield their faces and wings as well, though an earthling's eye couldn't see through the device.

In a second, Ares had hauled on his armor that covered his torso, forearms, and thighs. He handed me the ray gun, but I doubt it would do much harm on the armored Angels. They'd prepared and were armed to the teeth.

The whole legion had come just to capture me. Atlas was indeed beyond desperation.

Ares and I shared a look as we surveyed the situation. There was no escape route out of the villa embedded in the cave. There was only one entrance—the cave mouth—and now the front window.

When the High Prince of Angels had picked this place, he'd never thought of building a backdoor because he had wings and immense power. Now Ares and I had to pay for his arrogance and carelessness.

The legion besieged the Moonshade Villa and extended

beyond the forest.

Hatred burned in me. They had come for me, mere moments before Ares had been inside me. He'd just marked me as his, and I hadn't had time to savor the significance. I'd also just taken a leap of faith and come clean with him that I was his witch and he hadn't had time to think it over and react either.

Facing my immortal enemies and not seeing the slimmest chance of escaping, my fear rose as strongly as my hate, engulfing me like dark flames.

Ares put two of his fingers into his mouth, ready to summon the guardians.

I laid my hand on his arm. "No," I said.

He knew what I meant. I didn't want the guardians and his men to fly into the slaughter.

"I need you to escape while I hold them off," Ares said in a choked voice. "I need you to live. You'll take the chance."

He didn't plan to survive. Immense anguish and regrets flashed through his eyes. He thought he'd brought this to me. He thought he harmed his mate while all he wanted was to protect her—me.

I shook my head and gazed up at him, a thousand words in my eyes. He let go of his fingers, his face stricken with grief. He knew there was no chance for me—especially not for me—when a legion of Angels had come across the universe and light years to capture me.

No earthling army could overpower such a mighty legion. Only the elite battleships of the High Prince of All Angels could fight it. But the *ThunderSong* had returned to the Twilight Realm.

I looked up to the sky but didn't see any enemy spaceships. They had to keep the ships on the other side of the portal, not wanting to alert the High Prince. They planned to snatch me and run.

No one would come for us. No one would save us.

All I had was Ares, and he had me.

"Freyja, my true witch, my true mate," he said, his thumb moving across my cheek so gently, yet such rage storming in his eyes. Soon, even his fury would be ash as the legion of tens and thousands tore through us.

I half closed my eyes. Such was our fate.

The Oracle had led Ares to me. Had she seen this horror before us?

"When we can fight no more," I said, "you'll end me. You'll never let them catch me. The Dark Lord plans to feed on me and drain me dry."

"I won't let them have you," he said as he moved me further behind him.

As Merlin had said, my mate's primal instinct was always to protect me first and beyond anything.

An Archangel descended before the vanguard of the legion.

"Hello again, Princess," Eye-patch called. "Did I catch you at a bad time?" He leered at Ares, then at me, and started laughing.

Ares hadn't attacked as he was waiting for the best opening. Even though there was no hope, he still hoped I would escape and live a life without him.

"Shouldn't Dark Lord Atlas come in person?" I asked. "Oh, I forgot. He hasn't picked all of his pieces together."

Atlas could project his astral self to every corner of the universe before the Fey Empress and his heir shredded his essence. At the moment, Eye-patch was his eye. Through the link, he watched me from the far end of the hole where he hid like a coward.

"You're just like your vicious, rebellious uncle," Eye-patch said. "The High Prince destroyed our species, but at least you can be of use. With your sacrifice, Princess, the High Lord will return and rule again."

My heart skipped a beat. I'd come clean about being the First Witch, but I wasn't ready to let Ares know I was a Nephilim—the one and only Nephilim. I didn't want his last image of me to be tainted. But it was all out in the open. He now knew my most feared, darkest secret. He now knew I wasn't just a spawn to any Angel, but the monster Angel King, and the bloodline of the most powerful, despicable Dark Lord of All Angels.

Ares still shielded me behind him, his broad angelblade flashing before him, ready to draw the Angels' blood. And soon, I would fall under that blade, too, as he'd promised me.

At the revelation, Ares remained quiet. He couldn't look back at me while we faced our worst enemies, but from the slight rising and falling of his shoulders, I knew he wasn't unaffected by the news.

I gave Eye-patch a razor-sharp smile and stared into his eye with concentration. "I know you can see and hear me, Grandfather," I said in my most commanding voice. "Dispose of this vessel of yours. He offends my sight. I have no more tolerance to imperfection as you do."

I wouldn't mention that I was the cause of Eye-patch's maimed eye.

A chuckle boomed out of Eye-patch's throat, and I felt a penetrating gaze from him.

A power I hadn't felt before vibrated in the air.

Holy shit!

Atlas had taken charge of his vessel through light-years of

distance.

With shattering essence, the Dark Lord could still command such power. What would he do when he regained full strength? First, he'd return to Earth and deplete it for revenge.

I had only my pack before, but now I had more people I cared about deeply. I wouldn't let my grandfather destroy their planet.

My blood thrummed in my ear, but I held my ground.

The air crackled tightly. I knew the Angels felt their Dark Lord's signature power, for they all bowed their heads.

The only one who remained untouched was Ares.

He'd withdrawn half a step to hold my waist. My heartbeat returned to normal. His energy surged to me through our bond, replenishing and anchoring me.

He knew I had a plan, and he was aiding me, though he very much wanted to cut down my grandfather's possessed vessel, who hovered outside the broken window and stared down at me like a vulture waiting on a corpse.

I had no chance of getting away, but I could still manipulate Atlas to leave Ares alone. As soon as my mate was far away from the horde, I'd slice my throat good and deep with the angelblade hidden in my boot.

The Dark Lord would return empty-handed, except for my

bloodless corpse, which would be of no use to him.

"I sense great power in you, Freyja," Atlas said through Eye-patch. "You're indeed my granddaughter. I'm delighted and proud."

Of course he was delighted, he would harvest my essence. And the way he said my name creeped me out.

Ares clenched his teeth, pulling me tighter against him, his knuckles straining all white on the hilt of his sword. I subtly tried to untangle from him, but he only growled.

Idiot, I was trying to get him away from here. I wanted him to live.

"Since you've acknowledged me as your bloodline," I said. "I deserve respect and the privilege as the first and last Princess of All Angels. If you want to see me, Grandfather, all you have to do is to extend an invitation. Isn't it overdone by sending a horde of thousands to pick me up?"

Atlas laughed. "My sharp-tongued granddaughter! You're far more worthy than your useless father. However, as you said, you're the first and last Princess of All Angels—rare and precious, it would be only fitting to have the greatest army to escort you."

"Then we should be on our way." I sighed. "I don't want my boy toy to go with us, though I'm fond of him. I'm going to send him home, and then I'll pack."

Ares snarled. "You think I would leave you? They'll have to go through my dead body to get to you."

"Stop it," I hissed in a low voice and almost stomped on his foot for trying to ruin his only surviving chance. I couldn't bear to see him perish before me. I wouldn't allow it.

The vessel leered at us. "Child," he said, "you'll have to stay by my side for an eon to learn how to plot. My former heir is the only one who ever succeeded in overthrowing me, but not for long. Isn't the half-blood Dragonian your mate? His mark is all over you, just as your scent is all over him. He'll go with you to the end, as a good mate should do. My vessel wants to gut him, but I won't let him. However, I can't stop him from breaking your mate's bones one by one if you prove to be too difficult to manage on the journey to me."

It took less than five minutes for the ancient fuck to show his true colors. And I was a toddler—no, a fetus—compared to him when it came to dark schemes.

There was only one option left—fight the legion, take down as many as we could, and die in Ares' arms.

As soon as my decision was made, both Ares and I attacked Eye-patch in unison, determining to eliminate the Dark Lord's vessel first and hopefully hurt him in the process.

I aimed the ray gun toward his remaining eye, and Ares threw his dagger toward the enemy's heart.

Eye-patch flashed aside, ducking my energy beam. At the same time, he brought his broad sword up and sent Ares' dagger flying backwards.

The horde flapped their massive black wings excitedly at the start of a battle. Endless darkness rolled over the sky.

Fear churned in my stomach, but a rush of adrenaline pumped through my blood.

"Take the Princess!" Atlas ordered.

"Be my shadow," my mate ordered, meaning for me to fight behind him.

Ares transformed into his warrior form.

A nearly nine-foot-tall half-beast and half-giant man blocked the entrance of the broken window, wielding his angelblade to draw the first Angel blood.

The air tore open, and a battleship shaped like twin arrows burst through the portal and hovered above us in a slant angle.

The Reaper!

An intense light shot out and locked on me.

Ares bellowed and lunged to pull me out of the beam that would take me to the Reaper.

CHAPTER 16

Embrace Darkness

I kicked and screamed, but I was bound immobile as the spotlight suspended me in its column of beam toward the Reaper.

Ares slammed into the light again, but it sent him flying with its electric shock. His skin scorched, yet he immediately rolled up and charged at the light.

"Ares," I cried, tears streaming down my face, but I couldn't move a finger to wipe it off. "End me. Now."

He looked at me in horror, anguish twisting his near beastly face. He raised his sword, his hand trembling and his knuckles white on the hilt of the blade.

I gazed at him with tenderness and farewell. What wouldn't I give to have more time with him? Fate brought us together, so at least we could die in each other's arms.

He lowered his sword as tears flowed from the corner of his eyes. "I can't, love," he said. "I can never harm you."

"You promised me, Ares," I cried. "You can never let them take me!"

"They won't take you!" He kept stabbing at the beam to get to me while the light kept sending me up.

A burning sensation spread across my wrist. The silver bracelet Fia had given me flared a silvery light. Strange runes radiated on its surface, rippled through space, and shattered the beam that caged me.

I was no longer ascending; I was falling. Ares caught me and grabbed me to him.

Fia's words echoed in my head, "*Either I kill you or you wear it, so the old creep can't snatch you away easily. I can't allow him to have your power. I'm giving you a fighting chance. But before I leave Earth, you'll have to return the borrowed gift, or I'll hunt you down to the end.*"

Her magical bracelet had stopped the Reaper from taking me. I didn't think there was a chance in hell I would give this bracelet back to her. She could hunt me to the end of time, if she so desired.

How could she call this a fighting chance? I wished she was here to take a look around at what she deemed a chance.

But then, who would trust the wickedest witch in the

universe?

Eye-patch screamed and leveled his sword toward Ares. "Cut down the Dragonian beast and take the Princess!"

The Angel sentinels at the front row raised blades and charged toward us with battle cries.

Ares shoved me behind him and swept his sword toward the first Angel's neck. The Angel dodged and brought up his sword to meet the angelblade. The sharp sound of their crossing blades echoed in the villa. The second Angel tried to squeeze in, but Ares kicked him in the gut and sent him flying backwards. The Angel crashed into a row of his peers, a look of pure astonishment on his face. I bet he had never met a powerful earthling like Ares.

Pride swelled in my chest.

I played my sidekick role and shot my ray gun toward the Angels in a frenetic manner. I managed to shoot down quite a few from the sky and shouted my cheers when they fell. I knew we wouldn't last long. Our goal was to bring down as many enemies as we could until we could no longer fight.

Five sentinels emerged from the side. They'd entered through the cave's mouth. The defense system at the entrance had maimed several of them but failed to discourage the rest from charging in. I pressed my back against Ares as I shot at whoever showed up.

But there were too many of them, and their enhanced shield diffused my energy beam.

The sentinels waded over the bodies of their peers, competing to reach me. Every single one of them wanted to seize the Princess of All Angels for their Dark Lord.

Ares pierced his blade through an Angel's armor and buried into his chest. Three Angels were upon him the next. He slashed at them with his side angelblade, but as he pulled out his sword from the Angel's chest, another Angel sliced his leg.

Ares roared in fury as he swung his blood-tainted sword at that attacking Angel.

I couldn't join his fight. I had five Angels surrounding me in a half circle. My heart bled at the smell of my mate's rich-iron blood in the air.

Ares couldn't kill me when I'd begged. I would have to finish myself at the end. I had no battle experiences, but I had the leverage—none of the minions dared to bleed me before delivering me to their Dark Lord. I took full advantage of that and brought down a few more Angels.

Outside the window, Eye-patch called with my evil grandfather's eerie voice, "Princess, you've made your point. Now's the time to surrender. Quit being rebellious!"

What an ancient asshole!

Ares cut down more Angels, but he was wounded all over. They planned to bleed him out to weaken him.

Through our mating bond, every cut on his skin felt like a slice on me.

My heart ached. I kept shooting at my enemies and my angelblade stabbed wildly at them.

Fia had believed that I had a fighting chance and she hadn't said it lightly. Was the *ThunderSong* nearby? Did she and her mate plan to use me as bait?

After our encounter, somehow I could sense her magic.

She wasn't around. The *ThunderSong* wasn't close.

Ares and I might survive only if I could conjure my magic, but it was far beyond my reach. My dark beast was at the abyss of the ice lake.

"*Embrace your darkness, Witchling,*" Fia had lectured me without my invitation. "*Our kind never fears our great, terrible power.*"

I would try anything. I would release the darkest darkness in me. If my beast wanted to wear my skin from now on, so be it, as long as it could save my mate.

Ares wasn't slowing down even though blood gushed from his open wounds. But he would eventually bleed out.

Beast, I called. *Come and become me!*

There wasn't a stir. The she-beast didn't respond. She

refused to play.

So much for embracing the darkness!

Ferocious howls reached my ear from under the cliff. Had my pack followed me here?

Then roars thundered across the sky.

The guardians had come! Without Ares summoning them in order to spare them, they'd come for us. I glanced over the window. At the far end of the forest, our team broke through the opening, but then the Angels sealed the breach.

A dragon with jade-gold scales led the charge and tore a gap again. Astride the dragon sat Merlin. He'd also come for us, and with a legendary dragon!

The dragon spat fire, and Merlin sent his wind to push the fire further.

Warm tears wet my eyelids. I hadn't had any friends before. After Ares had kidnapped me, I'd gained many.

The Angels held their lines. I'd seen how they'd eliminated a whole race of dragons from another planet. Merlin's magic was great, but it couldn't destroy the Angel horde. Even with that knowledge, he'd still come for us.

To my surprise, a small Dragonian army, led by Caen, was attacking the left side of the Angel horde. Caen must have learned of the Angels' return and brought reinforcements that included the rest of the guardians in

Atlantis. Tyrone, the horned Dragonian whom Ares had banished, was among them. But if he was here, who was the traitor among us?

No time to ponder on that matter. Today, all of my friends would be slain.

The Angels were too mighty and many, and our power didn't stand a chance against this army. The ocean of hordes separated us. The Reaper opened fire on the guardians, and I saw one of them fall from the sky.

Beast, I summoned her urgently, my mind reaching her as I returned to the icy lake and broke the layers of ice for her to come out. *Become me. Take me. Do whatever you have to do and vanquish my enemies!*

A stir, and then nothing. She swam in the icy water, refusing to meet me.

I'd banished and caged her to the depth of the ice lake for decades.

This was her revenge. She would rather perish with me.

Ares fended off waves and waves of Angels, which only made them more excited and bloodthirsty. They hadn't seen an earthling resist them as he did, so they turned it into a brutal hunting game.

My ray gun and angelblade could no longer halt the swarm of the sentinels who poured in unceasingly through the cave of the mouth. And now, they had separated me from Ares.

As Ares withdrew to reach me, over a dozen Angels surrounded him from all sides.

An Angel used a corpse to shield himself from my ray gun, and another Angel disarmed me. It all seemed to happen within seconds, and before my mind could register it, the Angels cast a net over me.

The Reapers had failed to beam me up, so the Angels were using the conventional way to capture me. I pulled out my hidden dagger and slashed at the net to no avail. I couldn't cut through it. It had to be made of special materials.

"Freyja!" Ares bellowed furiously and lunged at the net, his eyes bloodshot at the sight of me being ensnared. He had dozens of cuts over him. Soon, he would fall under their swords.

There wasn't time for a proper farewell. People used to say "May we meet again," when they departed. What could I say to my Dragonian prince?

He'd just marked me as his moments ago. I'd even thought of giving up my freedom and living with him. We could have had a good life together—at least, the sex would always be fantastic.

I couldn't utter a word, but my eyes said it all—thousands

of words, regrets, and hopes.

"Freyja, hang in there, love!" he called, still refusing to let me go.

"Ares," I called back. "I'll see you in next life."

I would never be captured.

I was wild. I was free.

I turned the angelblade toward my throat. Ares lunged toward me, leaving his back to the Angels. Eye-patch thrust his blade into Ares' chest from behind, and an Angel shot a beam at my wrist before my dagger could slash a line across my neck.

I screamed Ares' name.

He dropped to his knees, gazing at me with love, sorrow, rage and pain. His hand reached the blade sticking out from his chest, trying to pushing it out. He still wouldn't give up. He still wanted to fight, wanted to protect me.

Through our mating bond, I knew he was heartbroken that he couldn't save me. The last light in his eyes was his profound, tender love for me that I'd been too late to catch up.

"No!" I screamed. "No! Don't die, Ares! Don't die!"

The Angels grabbed the tightened net and dragged me toward the open, broken window. Ares reached to grab the net when we passed by him, but an Angel kicked him down.

My enemies lifted me into the sky, leaving the cliff toward the Reaper.

"Freyja!" Ares roared. "Freyja!"

They were taking me away from my mate. Forever.

Ares was dying.

Rage and pain I hadn't known I was capable of vibrated in my every rebellious cell.

The instant I snapped, I let go of all of my fear. I knew what to do. If my beast wouldn't come to me, then I would go to her. I retreated back into myself, hurrying to make it to the lake. I dove through the shattered hole into the depth of the icy lake.

The water chilled my bones. The she-beast had suffered alone here for decades because of me. Now she stared at me without a word.

"Acknowledge it, claim it, own it, and command it," Merlin had said. He'd ridden the dragon and come for me. If I couldn't entice my beast out, Merlin would die with us. The guardians and Ares would soon perish. One of the guardians had gone down, and I didn't even know which one. I didn't even have room to grieve for him.

I've come to claim you, I declared, *as a part of me.*

You named me a monster and locked me up, she said.

For that I've paid dearly, I said. *I'm about to lose my*

mate. I can't lose him.

I'm the darkest darkness, she said, shifting forms between shape and shapeless, darker than midnight, darker than deep space, darker than the cores of the dark stars.

And I embrace you, I said with my heart.

The Angels had come to take me, my nightmares surrounding me.

I had nothing to lose except myself. And I had nothing to offer except myself.

When fear stared you in the face like an abyss, you better not stare back. You became it. My evil grandfather had just taken my last barrier, and now nothing stood between him and me.

My shapeless beast stalked toward me, her crimson eyes glowing and her breath dark. I opened my arms to welcome the menacing, mighty, and vengeful force.

In an instant, we merged. I arched my back with a gasp, and she sighed in satisfaction.

We were finally one.

And for the first time, I felt complete.

I felt marvelous and invincible.

Pure, dark power surged through me.

I was the ultimate predator in the universe.

And they treated me as a prey.

An unforgivable mistake.

Fury burst in me like a terrible storm from another universe; dark fire lit my skin and leapt, burning the net.

The Angels carrying the mesh yelped in alarm, their massive, black wings flapping. My dark fire rammed into them, burning their wings.

I did not fall.

Wind swirled around me, and a pair of blue-flamed wings burst from my back, arching high and beating.

"It can't be," Atlas's cries cut through Eye-patch's mouth.

Ares couldn't rise to his feet with the angelblade buried in his chest, but he was trying and waiting for Ventus to reach him, so he could come for me.

Ventus fought beside the blue dragon. Among the chaos, they'd nearly broken through the walls of the legion.

Ares stared up at me on the edge of the villa. I was afraid that he might see me as a winged monster, but there was only awe and wicked delight and adoration in his golden eyes. He knew I had come to power as the First Witch. He knew I would survive, though he might not.

I was his witch. He'd acknowledged me as such with no reservation.

An Angel dared raise his sword, ready to behead my mate.

I threw my head back, spread my arms, and roared,

"Behold the wrath of the First Witch!"

Red waves blasted from my body, surging toward the Angels who surrounded Ares. As my red wave hit, my immortal enemies inside the villa turned to skeletons, their flesh ripping off them. It passed through Ares, not harming him. The sword that had aimed to decapitate him dropped behind him.

The flame of my wings burned fiercely.

The battlefield froze. Everyone—my allies and enemies—turned to me with awe and fear. I flashed them a smile that had claws and teeth. Such power!

My darkness roared with joy.

My allies resumed fighting to get to Ares and me, and the Angel horde tried to put a safe distance between me and them. Who said that Angels were fearless?

"The Princess has the Red Plague!" Eye-patched cried. "Retreat!"

The horde followed the Reaper and sailed toward the portal that shimmered in the air.

For once, I could fight back with ease, and I was tired of being hunted. I would not allow them to leave.

I struck with my red wave, and bolts of lightning accompanied it. The Angels dropped from the sky like a mass of burned bats, their eyes bleeding and their shredded wings limp and useless.

My death touch was never my most lethal weapon—this was!

I was the First Witch.

"How does it feel to be impotent, Grandfather?" I laughed with sweet venom. "You'll stay that way until we come for you. I'm not the only one who wants your old ass."

Eye-patch shot toward the portal, but a thread of my red lightning coiled around him and dragged him back from the brink of the shimmering gate, bringing him back to me.

I stared into his eye, and the red abyss that was my eyes reflected back to me.

"Still want to harvest me, old clown?" I asked. "Here's my gift to help you return to your glory."

I slammed my red lightning into Eye-patch's chest.

He screamed. Atlas' furious shriek was a melody in my ear. I wished he could scream longer and feel the burn, but then Eye-patch blinked. He was himself again. His Dark Lord had abandoned his imperfect vessel. Incomprehensiveness and fear formed in his eye before my lightning diminished his every cell and returned him to skeleton, then dirt.

Earthlings had a saying: from dust we are formed, to dust we return.

Were Angels made of star dust?

I would ponder on that when my body wasn't aching so much.

It was the first time I'd used my most lethal magic and I didn't know how to take it easy. Besides, I couldn't take it easy when I had a hostile force to burn.

My magic consumed me.

My last red wave rolled across the horizon, red lightning sparking faintly at its vanguard before whimpering out. There were no more Angels in sight. Reaper and a few Angels had escaped through the portal. Pity.

I turned toward Ares. Merlin and his dragon had reached him. The druid knelt beside my prince, tending to him, and the dragon guarded the entrance, his massive form blocking part of my sight of Ares.

My heart burned with need and desperation for my mate and my stomach churned with acid fear. Would Merlin be able to save him? I wouldn't know how to live in a world without Ares.

Intense pain, pride, and amazement were etched on Ares' face, and his amber eyes, though dimming now because of the loss of the blood, never left me.

I had to go to him. I had to fly back to him.

But the flame winked out, and my wings vanished.

I had no magic, strength, or no energy left. I plummeted toward the ground.

"Freyja! Ventus!" Ares roared, blood pouring out of his mouth.

Stop yelling, idiot, I wanted to say.

Something snatched my body before I hit layers of Angel corpses at the bottom of the cliff.

Ventus had me in his huge claws.

Hello, Witchling, he said in my mind.

You and your brethren should address me as The Great and Terrible First Witch of Earth from now on, I advised. *I believe I've earned the title today.*

It's an inside joke, right? he asked as he soared up toward the villa.

"Hey, Dragon." Ventus said. "Move aside and let my mistress pass."

The blue dragon sent me a cautious look, gave Ventus an evil eye, and puffed out a stream of fire. But she swept her tail of golden-blue scales and allowed us to approach Ares and Merlin.

What an attitude! Ventus murmured, but for a second, he was staring at the dragon's splendid scales with envy.

Ventus gently laid me beside Ares.

I knew how I looked—ashen face, lifeless dull eyes, dry

and chapped lips. On top of that, my flaming hair was splayed around my head in wild tangles.

Merlin had extracted the angelblade from Ares' chest and miraculously stopped his bleeding.

I sobbed in relief, yet my fear lingered.

"Freyja," Ares whispered, "I'm sorry I couldn't save you, but you saved yourself and us. You returned to me."

"Where else can I go without you?" I asked weakly.

He reached for me, his thumb tracing across my cheek, and his energy burst in me like a beam of sunlight.

Merlin grabbed Ares' wrist and lifted it off my skin. Both of us growled.

"Not now," the druid said. "She'll absorb your life force. She can't control herself when she's depleted."

"Then let my mate have it!" Ares snarled. "I won't let her deplete."

"There will be a time you'll need to give her energy, but that time is not now," Merlin insisted.

My dull eyes warned Ares to back off.

A humming of machines grew louder in the air.

To my horror, a fleet of Reapers tore through the rift of the portal.

Revenge was a bitch. Atlas had known that I was worn out, and he was determined to take me today. There was no chance in hell I could get up again and throw my power at another horde.

I'd timed it wrong. The horde of tens and thousands of Angels had been the distraction. Atlas' true force had been waiting behind the portal to strike me. They'd waited until I'd emptied myself of my magic. When they captured me, they would put me inside a glass coffin to prevent me from regenerating until they tossed me onto the operation table before their Dark Lord.

I thought we'd won the battle. In the end, I was but a fetus against an ancient serpent.

A flash of dark lighting pierced through half of the sky.

My heart leapt.

ThunderSong materialized. I'd never been so happy to see High Prince Seth's symbol of a black lightning bolt slashing across the ship's hull.

ThunderSong led a fleet and came to meet the Reapers.

A formidable Angel stood beside Gabriel by the view window, his golden wings arching behind him and his eyes burning with furious black lightning.

"Fire!" the High Prince of All Angels bellowed.

Fia, who leaned against Gabriel, tilted her head to give the High Prince an evil eye, probably annoyed at his loudness, before turning toward me with a wicked grin.

I wasn't in the mood to return even a half smile. I didn't even have energy left to stab a finger in her direction to accuse her of using me as bait.

What a wicked world! And I stared into its delightful face as the real battle broke out.

My last thought was Ares.

And my flaming wings.

I was once glorious.

I was loved.

CHAPTER 17

The Matehood

My eyes fluttered open. Warm sunlight sifted through the silk curtain adorned with drawings of a phoenix.

Immediately, I knew I was in the Silver Palace of Mysth from a memory.

The suite smelled of spring blossoms. Outside the window, the landscape of green, violet, and blue sprawled to the red forest.

A sob escaped me. My mother had stayed in this room and looked out the window at the red and silver trees before she'd been sent to the monster Angel King.

A flute sounded near, bringing joy and sorrow at once.

A large hand touched my face before I turned to search for Ares.

Another sob of joy and relief caught in my throat.

Ares had survived.

His knuckles traced across my cheek, and my need for him rose greatly.

"How do you feel, love?" he asked.

I blinked at him. I'd been used to him yelling at me, "Freyja, stop it." Or "Freyja, must you screw it up?" It felt strange that he now called me love and used his enticing, velvet voice on me as if all of a sudden I was made of paper and glass.

"How long have I been out?" I asked.

"Three nights and two days, love," he said. "Seeing you like this drove me out of mind."

Was my name going to be 'love' from now on? I frowned at him.

"What displeases you, love?" he asked. "Do you feel pain? I'll send Einarr to fetch the healers."

So the advanced human also lived. What about Lucas, the guardians, and the others?

I seized his arm to stop him from rising to call Einarr or anyone. I didn't want him to leave me for a second.

He sat back on the edge of the bed. "I won't leave you, love."

"How's your chest wound?" I asked. "Let me see it."

He unbuttoned his shirt. "I regenerated well with Merlin's

help. The Fey aided you with their Earth magic."

A jagged scar was blunt on his chest. I vowed that the Dark Lord would pay for it one day.

"The blade missed my heart by an inch," Ares said, grabbing my hand and pressing it against his warm chest. His strong heartbeat thumped against my palm. Feeling the pulse was intoxicating, not only did it mean that he was a live, but for a Nephilim who carried a death touch, who didn't inspire a heart to beat but instead to stop, the thrumming under my hand was one of the greatest feelings in the world.

"It now beats even faster and stronger for you," he said.

I stared at his chest, his muscles rippling, his heat radiating, and his scent dominating.

Lust sprang in my veins.

"Want me again, my little mate?" Ares asked, his voice turning from smooth velvet to rough and husky.

I swallowed, but I needed to know if everyone was okay first.

Ares seemed to read my thoughts. He leaned against the headboard and gathered me up onto his lap, his arms sliding around me possessively. I liked him being clingy. I liked it even more when I felt his huge bulge under my bottom. I wouldn't object if he thrust it up inside me now.

"The Fey and the High Prince's Fallen Angels came in

time," Ares said. "My main army also arrived. Prince Seth's fighters blew off a fleet of Reapers. *ThunderSong* chased into the portal to hunt the rest. The wicked woman and her Angel mate led the hunt. The Dark Lord's force won't be a threat for a while, but we must always stay alert."

His cock pressed so hard against me that it was torment not to have it fill me inside. We could talk while he fucked me, so he could soothe the fire in me. However, it might not be the right thing to do while fury and grief swirled in his eyes.

"We lost Glacies and Jericko," he said.

An ache squeezed my heart. The guardian of ice had become my friend. He'd liked me. He'd tried to put out my cursed fire. He'd defended me. He would no longer be among us, but he'd always be missed.

Jericko was the one who had the bluest skin among the Dragonians. We hadn't gotten along, but he had fought hard for Ares.

"I saw Tyrone coming back with Caen to fight the horde," I said.

Ares nodded, stroking my hair. "He found out Jericko was the traitor." He shook his head in sadness. "Two thirds of the men Caen brought perished. All of our surviving men are still recovering from their battle wounds. The Fey healers have being using their magic to help heal them."

His men didn't have Ares' amazing regenerating ability.

"Where's Merlin?" I asked.

"Miss him?" he asked. Thought he knew he was the only man I ever wanted, there was still a hint of jealousy in his voice. He couldn't help it. Our mating bond demanded our absolute devotion to each other.

"I miss this." I swayed my hips on his erection and he gasped, his eyes turning molten gold. "But I need to ask you first: do you have a problem with me being the First Witch?"

"I've been processing this for three days now," he said. "You led me on a wild goose chase. You made a fool out of me."

"When I told you I was the First Witch the first time, and you said, 'Sure, and I'm the Dark Lord of All Angels.' Remember?" I winced at merely mentioning my grandfather, but there was no longer an option of avoiding talking about my bloodline.

"You're an expert at mixing truth and lies," he said. "No one on Earth has the mind to sort them all out. First, you said the witch was heading east."

"Didn't I head east to the Twilight Realm at that time?"

"You said she was the opposite of you—plain, old, and uncreative."

"Because you prayed she was the opposite of me."

Ares sighed. "I don't blame you. I should have known, but I was an idiot. I brought all this suffering to us because I was so fucking blind. When I first touched you, I was on fire, and every cell in me came alive. I wouldn't feel that way if you weren't my mate. I've never felt that kind of heat toward any female. My instincts screamed that you were mine, but I tried to listen to my cold reasoning. All the signs were there—your emerging magic, my immunity to your death touch, Merlin's and the guardians' reactions to you, and the ancient elemental tongue you could speak—but I kept looking the other way. Whenever I'm around you, I truly feel home. Atlantis is mine, but it never feels like home to my soul. When I thrust in you the first time, I blinked out of my existence, because you've become my whole world. Yet I still believed the First Witch was on the other side of the horizon while you were in front of me all this time. I deserved all of the torment and more."

He'd seen all of the signs, but he always caught up with them a step slower because of his belief in the Oracle's promise. Didn't they say prophecy was a double-edged sword?

"Will you forgive me, Freyja, my love?" Then he added, "I've never asked for anyone's forgiveness since I never needed to. But you're my mate, so I'll do this for you."

The prince was always the prince, wasn't he? He sounded like he was doing me a favor. He would have to make a lot of compromises living with me, and I would have to do the same.

I sighed. Being Ares' queen would take the work of Earth and the Heavens.

As for forgiveness, he didn't need to ask for that. He'd protected me. He'd always put my life above his. In the end, he'd chosen me above all—the witch and his kingdom.

Now was my turn to ask the tough question. "Does it mean you're fine with me being the last spawn of the monster Angel King? You hate him and the Angels more than anything, and I have Angel blood in my veins."

"Why must I care what blood runs in you, love?" he asked in puzzlement. "You're *you*, my Freyja. I wouldn't have marked you as my one and only mate if I don't love you."

My heart skipped a beat, then pumped furiously. He'd been calling me love, but it was different than claiming to love me.

"Do you really mean that? You don't despise me for being a Nephilim—an abomination?"

"You aren't an abomination, Freyja," he snarled. "Anyone who calls you that will fall under my sword! You don't realize how beautiful and special you are. You're one of a kind, my cunning witch."

"But you said I forever annoyed the hell out of you."

"That too." He kissed my lips, gentle and hard at the same time. "I'll have to live with that. You're the only female made for me."

"I don't want to be one of a kind."

"Is that why you hid your true identity from me?"

"That and more," I said. "I was also mightily pissed at you."

"Are you still?"

"It depends on what you'll do next," I said sultrily and regarded his tanned torso, my eyes traveling from his massive shoulders to his hard chest and muscled stomach. His trousers hung low, and a trail of golden hair disappeared under it suggestively.

His erection grew harder and larger beneath me.

I licked my lips. My panties were soaked with my arousal. He gazed down at me in amusement, lust a dark storm in his golden eyes.

"You're recovering," he said. "I won't hurt you, no matter how much I want you now."

"Hasn't Merlin told you that your touch can energize me?"

"That and more," he said. "He said I'm electricity to you."

"So what are you waiting for? I need a little reboot now."

Ares slanted his mouth on mine, and sparks crackled and ignited between us. He deepened the kiss and slammed his tongue against my hard palate. A moan escaped from my throat, and I grabbed his hair.

A raw, guttural sound rumbled from his chest. He pulled my gown off me and caressed my breasts roughly. I ground my ass against his hardness.

"You drive me crazy, my gorgeous little monster," he said huskily. Even his voice sent a shiver of pleasure down my spine. His hands moved to grab and cup my butt, and his mouth took over where his hand used to be, enveloping my taut nipple. His suckling made my blood run hot and cold, then hot again.

"Ares," I whispered as I yanked his cock out of his trousers.

Its silky head jerked forward. Ares' lips left my breast. He liked the way I looked at his cock. A moist bead emitted from the slit in response.

"It wants your sweet pussy," he said, his voice slurry. The prince was in the grip of lust. "How bad do you want me to fuck you?"

"So bad," I breathed, "but I want to taste you first."

His eyes brightened. Ares opened his legs wide, his cock shooting straight for the treat.

I bent down, my tongue flicking out and licking the liquid from his crown. He sucked in a sharp breath. He tasted so good that I was on him again in an instant, my tongue tracing the column of his length from the base, all the way up to the head in one slow, languorous movement. When my tongue reached the head, it swept over the thick ring of his crown.

Ares groaned blissfully.

My teeth nipped his cock, and he barked a series of curses and bucked his hips up.

Only then did I take his shaft into my mouth, gliding up and down and suckling him mercilessly.

"You're gonna make me come, Freyja," he inhaled and exhaled, his hand tangled in my thick hair. "You're everything to me, and I need to fuck you now."

I released his cock and smacked my lips.

Ares lifted me until I was practically sitting on his face. His mouth devoured me, his tongue thrusting into my heated channel. Pleasure rippled through my inner walls and spread further and further. With a nip on my inner thigh, he released me and put me down on bed, bending my knees to my chest to give him uncontested access to my bare sex.

He leaned in and thrust his cock into my depth, right until

he hit the hilt, until his heavy balls slammed into my bottom.

The first thrust was the most glorious, and it got only better from there.

He stared at our joined flesh, lust making his face beastly, which aroused me like no other. He picked up the pace and fucked me faster and harder. I wanted to propel up to meet his plunging, but he pinned me right there, in absolute control. The prince merely wanted me to enjoy the ride.

"Such a hot, tight pussy," he groaned, pulling out a little and driving back in hard. "The best I've ever had. The only one I'll have from now on. Your pussy will always be there for me to fuck whenever I want and however I want."

Always be there for him to fuck? Want to bet on it? The prince still believed that he could take whatever he wanted, as he was used to. I would teach him a lesson about that later. Now the pleasure was just too much for me to gather my wits to challenge him.

He groaned erotically at the pleasure.

"You're going to make me come in a second, little mate," he said, clenching his teeth. "I can barely contain myself. Oh, Earth!" He thrust into my depth, then stilled. "I'm going to slow down now to savor you. We have forever."

He adapted to move slowly and causally in me, as if he decided to take a nap basked in the afternoon sunlight, but it only made my lust boil.

I tried to move my hips up to help him correct his course, but he pinned me in position. He would drive me mad if he kept teasing me.

"I need you to go faster," I demanded.

"But, love, I want to make love to you. This is the way to do that, in case you don't know," he said, pulling out a little and taking his time to penetrating me.

That was enough.

Let's see how he could sustain it.

I inserted a finger into my mouth, my other hand fondled my breast, and I let out a string of my most lusty moans as I writhed beneath him.

"I can't get enough of your big cock," I said breathlessly. "It fits my pussy perfectly. Your every hard thrust eases my aches."

A moment ago, he was trembling from restraining himself from fucking me any harder. He no longer had the restraint. My seduction had worked, and his need to drive in me at his natural speed won over his determination of slow sampling.

He let go and thrust in me with abandon, his muscles rippling on his torso at his powerful moves.

"Yes, harder! Deeper! Faster!" I cried.

"You asked for it, woman!" He quickened his thrusting to

a fever pitch.

I moaned louder at the intense pleasure that rocked me senseless. I'd never imagined that mating could be so spectacular.

"Want more, my lusty female?" He poured his strength into me, hard and raw.

My core ignited, the heat liquefying.

"Is it good for you, my little mate?" he asked, moving his hips clockwise, and a new kind of sensation hit my nerve endings.

"You can do better, Dragonian," I purred, freeing my legs from his binding and wrapping them tightly around his waist.

"You should have told me you're my mate on our first encounter," he said, "so we wouldn't have been tormented for so long. I wanted to fuck you at first sight. I wanted to pin you against a tree and thrust into you so hard from behind, with your bountiful breasts in my hands. I fantasized fucking your pussy so hard that you'd cry."

He pounded harder between my thighs as if punishing me for delaying his pleasure for too long.

I lifted my hips to meet his rapid thrusts. "You never asked the right question, Prince," I said between moans. "You were determined to exclude me from the beginning, even though, instinctively, you wanted me since I was your rightful mate."

"So you punished me all the way?"

"You think this is punishment?" I purred. "Should we stop then?"

"There's no chance in hell I'll stop. Neither will you," he said, plunging into me with his hybrid's will and power. His movements became a blur; his muscles rubbed me roughly and powerfully.

"Oh, Ares!" I cried for mercy. The wave was coming, pushing me to the edge.

His cock became as rigid and hard as the granite. His coming approached in a tidal wave. His mouth dropped to the mating mark he'd claimed on the base of my neck and his tongue licked it.

"Mine!" he roared. "Mine forever!"

His body tensed like a coiled whip before he released it. The prince hit the very depth of me and pumped his seed into my well. I let go as I fell off the cliff and landed on the high waves that came to meet me.

As our orgasms throbbed and echoed each other's, our mating bond radiated like the sun.

"My mate, my love, my future queen," he said, emptying himself completely into me.

~

Afterwards, I pressed my face on his chest, my hand circling his bellybutton lazily.

The Fey Empress would send for me soon, but now I wanted to spend all of the idle time with Ares.

"We'll talk to the Fey about the cure," he said. "As soon as we have it, we'll leave for Atlantis. I need to go see my father."

"You can leave me here."

He growled. "I'll never leave you behind. A Dragonian doesn't separate from his mate."

Would his temper ever ease?

"You're only a half Dragonian."

"It doesn't matter. Wherever I go, you go."

I hoped he wouldn't say more about being his shadow or him leading and me following. We'd just had hot sex. I wasn't in a biting mood.

"You'll sleep in my arms every night and wake up every morning with my cock buried deep inside you. I'll fuck you whenever I get a chance, and you'll scream my name when you come."

It sounded enticing. But he got the most out of it.

"But—" I started.

"You'll like Atlantis," he coaxed. "We'll live in the

western dome of the golden tower. You'll have everything you ever want. And your wolves can live in our garden."

"My pack likes to hunt. I don't think they like pretty gardens."

"Everyone needs to learn to make a compromise in order to live in peace and harmony, which includes your wolves."

Good luck talking to my pack about that, especially the she-wolf Lenka.

His tone softened as he glanced down at my sour expression.

"If you worry about the wolves hunting the servants," he said, "I'll have the guardians to keep them in check. You don't need to worry about a thing from now on, love."

Maybe other females wanted that—not to worry about anything, but that wasn't what I had in mind for my life. I hadn't had time to process all of the changes and hadn't had a chance to come up with a plan for my future.

"So both my wolves and I just got ourselves a huge, gilded cage?" I said.

"It's not a cage. If you insist on it being a cage, I'm living in it with you, aren't I?

"I don't like my life to be any different than before, Ares. I like to roam freely."

"Yes, in my—our palace and our garden. Even in Atlantis,

when the elite guards escort you."

Again, a cage.

"You aren't just the wolf girl now, Freyja," he said. "Now everyone knows that you're the First Witch. You've demonstrated your great power and made a declaration to the world."

"I didn't exactly announce my debut," I said. "I was merely trying to survive."

"You did well, love," he said. "But now that we've mated, things will be different. I'll give you time to adjust." He raised his torso to plant a quick kiss on my lips to assure me and flashed me a grin. "I'm a patient man."

He'd never once demonstrated his patience ever since I'd met him.

But if this was the beginning of a negotiation, I needed to get a better deal.

"It's for me to decide where I go, sit, or sleep," I said. "Even though we've mated, it doesn't give you the right to decide everything for me. And you don't get to determine my future path either."

"Your future is with me," he said, then at my dark look, he asked, "How about we make decisions together?"

He was offering to co-rule if I became his future queen. I darted my eyes slowly as I considered it.

"I love you, Freyja. I'll make things work for you, for us. Tell me, what do you want to do next? Where would you like to go?"

"I'm thinking of returning to my forest home."

"Then I'll go live with you and your pack."

"But you have a kingdom to run."

"What is a kingdom to me without you? Since you won't live me with in Atlantis, then I'll have to go to the place you choose."

I gazed at him. He meant it. He was going to give up his kingdom for me. And it wasn't the first time. When he'd chosen me over the witch, he'd given up the new, phantom kingdom the Oracle had said the First Witch was going to bring to him.

I still had no idea how I was going to do that. I was still Freyja. I had no money, no army, and definitely no kingdom in my palms. Though I wasn't hunted at the moment, my grandfather would never give up coveting my power. He would return to harvest me at the next possible opportunity. Danger and threat would always be around me.

Ares knew, yet he still chose me.

I wouldn't live without him either. I'd realized that when I'd watched the Angel pierce Ares' chest with an angelblade.

"I'll live in your golden palace with you," I said. "I'll go to Atlantis."

He blinked. "Wasn't that what I proposed in the first place?" Then he shook his head. "All right then, I'll always ask you before making decisions for us."

"Ask nicely and we'll make decisions together," I said.

He slid his hand to cup my sex. "Should I ask first and nicely now?"

Heat rose in me, but I didn't need to raise a finger to seduce him. The prince wasn't any more disciplined than I, although he'd constantly demanded I learn it when we'd been on the road. His cock expanded to full length, harder than a rock.

Before I rode him again, I needed to make sure one last thing.

"You do realize that even though I'm the First Witch," I said, "I'm nothing like what the Oracle said. I have nothing to offer you."

"You have everything to offer me," he said. "Just look at your hot body."

His hand started rubbing my sex, and his eyes darkened with desire. We were insatiable toward each other.

"Is my body the only thing you value?" I hissed.

He sighed, laying on his side and pulling me against his chest.

"You're the First Witch on Earth, Freyja," he said. "Do you know what it means for the future of our kingdom?"

"I don't see my being the First Witch having anything to do with the future of a kingdom."

"You don't see it now, my silly mate. We're the first powerful hybrids and the beginning of a whole new race. Our children will be superior in every aspect. They'll have my strength and your magic. You'll produce many little witches and warlocks with my enhanced genetic makeup, little wife. They'll dominate the Earth. The pure-blood advanced humans won't lead, nor will the Dragonians. The Fey can hide inside their walls. The world will evolve and they will be left behind and forgotten. But our offspring will lead Earth to a new era. We're the start of that great future—you and me. That's what the Oracle meant. That's why she sent me to find you."

So his ambition was back. So quickly?

I narrowed my eyes. "Aren't you giddy that you got yourself a breeder?"

"No!" He placed his large hand at the back of my skull and maneuvered my head so he could peek into my eyes. "You know what's in my heart, Freyja. I would give up anyone and anything for you. You're above my kingdom and myself. How do you want me to prove that to you?"

He'd proved that when he'd thrown himself at my cursed fire and the blades between me and the Angels.

I pressed a hand on the new scar on his chest. "You don't need to prove anything."

"Don't you want my young, our young?" he asked.

"I'm too young for that," I said. "I haven't really lived yet." Thanks to my evil grandfather and his Angel hunters.

"You can start living the life you want and I'll be with you every step of the way. We'll share everything. As for children, we don't need to make a plan for that right now. We have time. One day, you'll beg me to have our super babies."

I blushed. I wondered why I still felt shy sometimes. I'd finally known a man intimately and tried so many different sexual positions.

He smiled, obviously liking my pinkish face, and kissed both my cheeks.

"I don't see how I'll beg to nurse your—our—babies and change their diapers!" I said.

A laugh danced in his eyes. "When the time comes, you'll fight me for that."

He'd have to wait a long time for that. The heat between my legs spread and I needed to fuck him again. I was utterly addicted to the feel of his cock inside me.

He read my desire. "Take what you want, my female," he

said roughly.

He stroked my breasts; his every touch was flame in my blood, and my mind shorted. The meaningful conversation was over.

"I need a bath," I said.

"That I can arrange," he said, sweeping me up and carrying me toward the bathing chamber.

The tub was already filled with warm water, but Ares was in no rush to help wash me since he was more interested in caressing, exploring, and teasing the flesh between my thighs.

Primal, pure male desire distorted his handsome face.

While the wildfire coursed through my veins, he lifted my leg. My folds opened for him enthusiastically. Ares aimed the thick head of his cock at my entrance and glided in from the side, stretching and filling me.

I pushed my ass back to glide along his length, and he let me enjoy that for a minute or so before taking control again and driving his enormous, hard cock into me with brutal strength.

Wolves howled outside the door, led by my beta Blaez, echoed by the red she-wolf Lenka.

My pack was here? How had that happened?

"They tracked you and found you when the Dark Lord's

legion came for you," Ares said, not slowing his thrusting. "They climbed the cliff to try to get to you and tore into your enemies' wings on the way down, though they were no match for the Angels."

"I told them to go north and preserve themselves," I said, arching my back to take him in deeper.

"They wouldn't leave you," he said. "By the way, I haven't had a chance to tell you that they've accepted me as your mate." He shook his head. "Ventus said that they call me your consort."

My wolves weren't exactly easygoing when it came to the outsiders.

I narrowed my eyes on my arrogant, powerful mate. "How? What did you do to them?"

He grinned. "Well, it took a little extra work of course, a bit of bribe, plus some degree of necessary intimidation. They're cunning, just like you. They're also practical."

My pack called again outside.

Wait, I'm coming, I ordered them. *And don't scratch the door.*

They flashed pictures in their heads.

They'd been playing with the blue dragon and flying alligators in the Twilight Realm's most enchanting red forest. They weren't too impressed with the winged beasts, but they tried to get along with them.

Well done, I commented. *But all things considered, do not call them winged beasts to their faces. Especially do not call the guardians flying alligators. They're proud and sensitive, and they're more, just as you are more.*

The wolves agreed after a bargain, and then they flashed a message.

The Fey Empress had sent them to fetch Ares and me.

Ares quickened his thrust in urgency. "I'll take time fucking you for the whole night when we get to Atlantis, love."

We came together in a tremble and I sank my fingernails into his thighs.

So much for helping me bathe.

CHAPTER 18

Twilight Realm

Sunset lingered above the ancient forest that shielded the Fey's ivory city.

Silver blossoms and red leaves floated in the wind and dropped like a dream.

The rich, fickle texture of the time flowed differently in this realm than in other places on Earth. With the potent magic in me, I could sense the pulse of Earth magic—alive, fresh, and scented like the finest wine.

Wind passed by, calling me. I shivered, and Ares thought I was cold and wrapped a protective arm around me.

My wolves howled with delight, leading us toward the Empress' royal garden. Einarr, Lucas, Caen, Boomer, and Tyrone had all joined us. The guardians flew in the wicked wind above the magical forest with the dragon.

Just as I wondered where Merlin was, we reached the Fey's exquisite garden.

The druid was conversing with a girl wearing a crown of blue diamonds. She looked about nineteen and would forever look that way.

The Empress of Mysth turned to me, her eyes the color of moonlight streaming in a glass of whiskey that held fire of passion.

Goddess Rhea's favorite immortal daughter.

Two powerful Angel brothers had started the civil war over her. I stole a glance at Ares, but he didn't seem to be that impressed. Pride rose in me—he was utterly, completely mine.

His men, however, weren't immune to Earth's beauty. They stared at her, dumbstruck, until a growl rose somewhere.

The Emperor.

He was perfection. His eyes were a piercing ice grey. His glorious, golden wings arched behind him and radiated in the dusk.

My father had torn out the wings of the High Prince, but the Fey Empress had healed her mate with her great Earth magic. It was once tragic but now poetic that he had lost his wings for her and she had given them back to him.

Ares checked on me to see if I was touched by the High Prince's glacial, lethal beauty.

I sent him a lopsided grin. I also was utterly his.

Empress Rose sent her husband a mildly chiding look and Ares turned to give his men a sharp glare, and all of them opted to stare ahead at nothing. Chastening achieved.

"Prince Darken, we meet again," the Fey Empress said with a smile, then turned to me. "Freyja, welcome—"

Two Angel toddlers shot straight toward me like arrows.

Ares moved to step in front of me, ready to meet their impact, but I pressed a hand on his arm to stop him. I'd recognized them as the Emperor and Empress' twins.

The little Angels flew around Ares and me in speedy circles, their miniature wings beating rapidly in the air.

I opened my mouth to warn them, but Empress Rose said, "Your magic won't harm them." Then she called out, "Elijah! Daniel! Stop pestering your cousin."

Cousin? So the Fey Empress knew who I was. She wasn't going to kill me. She was fulfilling her vow to my mother.

But her warning to her children didn't seem to have any effect, since every time they flew to my side they would tug my hair and giggle. I guessed they were fascinated by its flaming color.

Ares clenched his fists then released them. He would fight

an adult Angel at any time, but facing two naughty fat toddlers, what could you do? He was also afraid of hurting the twins and blowing my chance of getting the cure from the Empress.

The Emperor came to my aid, faster than lightning, and plucked the twins out of their high speed stream. He held each of them under one of his arms.

The little Angel kicked and screamed, tiny fists waving. The High Prince wasn't yielding. He ordered in a stern voice, "Do you want a hard spank on your little butts? I can deliver it nicely!"

Empress Rose winced. "Seth, be careful with their wings."

That concern immediate gave the twins an idea. They cried, urgently calling for their mother.

"Mother, Father hurt my left wing," one of the twins called. "I'll look like a chicken if he breaks another pretty feather."

"My tummy hurts, Mommy!" the other twin joined. "Father must have left bruises."

Their father grated. "You're Angels. You don't bruise like the mortals!"

"Consort, will you take it easy?" the Empress raised her voice.

The Emperor sighed. "We talked about parenting."

"Parenting is about loving and caring," the Empress said in a clipped tone. She looked like she wanted to lunge at her husband to rescue her sons.

"*Eroma*, we can't keep spoiling them," the High Prince softened his tone. "They'll grow up into two fiends and antagonize the whole universe." It was strange to see such a formidable Angel being so careful and gentle with his mate, but then he also called her his thorn as an endearment. "Sometimes we must discipline them for the greater good."

"We can think about the greater good when our twins are a bit older, husband," the Empress said. "They've just learned how to fly."

"It'll be too late then," the Emperor sighed. "They must learn discipline at early age."

Ares nodded in agreement and squeezed my hand meaningfully. He was still eager to have offspring with me. But wasn't it too soon to think about parenting? I shook my head. Dragonians loved to plan things way ahead.

The twins kept whining about their other small body parts hurting.

"Heavens!" the Emperor shouted. "You're Angels. You're fucking stronger than steel, even though you're a pair of insufferable toddlers. Stop manipulating your poor, softhearted mother!"

"Language, Consort," the Empress said.

The twins only screamed louder for their poor, softhearted mother.

The Empress rose to her feet and stalked to her mate, her skirt flowing in the breeze.

Two Angel nannies appeared, and the High Prince tossed his twins—one to each nanny—and they retreated back to the palace.

The High Prince moved toward his mate, his arm wrapping around her possessively as he gave her a tender kiss, and she kissed him back.

Just like that, their domestic crisis was resolved.

One of the twins broke free from the nanny and shot toward the sky, his little wings flapping enthusiastically. "Come and get me. I dare you, big birds!"

The Angel nanny chased into the sky.

The other nanny gripped the remaining toddler tightly as the little one struggled to get free and attempted to escape.

The Emperor and Empress stared up toward the sky. The Emperor looked like he wanted to shoot up to go after his son, but when he glanced at his mate and us, he decided to stay to guard her.

"Come, Freyja," Empress Rose said, reaching for my hand.

I hesitated, but Merlin had said the Fey Empress and my uncle were also immune to my death touch because they were too powerful. The Empress gave me a knowing smile. I relaxed.

The Empress held my hand and led me to the oval table in the center of the garden, a gesture to show her acceptance. She was merciless to her enemies, but she was always good to her people. My mother had been her people.

A Fey steward led Ares' men toward the refreshments in the courtyard.

This would be a private conversation for a small group of people.

Merlin stood and greeted Ares, "Prince Darken, your father sends his greetings."

His father sent his greetings from the death bed?

Ares nodded. "We'll head back to Atlantis tomorrow. Please join us, Merlin."

Merlin inclined his head an inch.

The guardians would be thrilled to fly with the she-dragon a little longer. I believed that Ventus was smitten with the dragon.

The druid smiled back at me before he settled back in his seat. "Freyja, good to see you again."

Empress Rose let me perch near her and Ares lounged into

a seat beside me. The Emperor lingered nearby, one eye on his twins, and the other on his mate.

Ares placed his arm around me possessively. My Dragonian prince had become quite clingy.

"I heard that you got wings, Freyja," Empress Rose said.

"Only in my battle form," I said. "I won't be able to conjure them otherwise." I'd tried when the twins had tugged at my hair. I'd wanted to see how they would react when they saw the burning wings. They would probably run from me and come back later to harass me more. But facing two little naughty Angels couldn't kick me into a red rage, so my wings wouldn't manifest.

"Flaming wings," Merlin said. "Never saw anything like that."

The Emperor snapped his head toward me. "Your great-grandfather had flaming wings," he said. "You must get them from him."

I blinked. I had so little knowledge of my ancestry.

"Atlas assassinated him to take his power," added the High Prince of All Angels.

"Charming family," I said.

A faint smile tugged at the Angel Prince's lips. And suddenly, his perfect statue-like face wasn't icy anymore.

"It can be learned," said the High Prince. "I'll show you

how to summon them before you leave."

He was actually a nice guy, not like what the rumors said.

"My home is yours, Freyja," the Empress said, "as it was once your mother's. You're welcome to stay here forever. No Angels can hunt you in my realm."

"My future queen will live with me in her rightful place in Atlantis," Ares cut in, not so subtly. Then he realized that he needed to ask me and turned to me. "Will you, Freyja?"

"Yeah, but—" I said. This was another opportunity to drive a hard bargain, but what should I bargain for?

"There's no but on this matter," Ares said. "We can negotiate on other things."

Merlin looked at us with an amused smile that said "Didn't I tell you this would be interesting?"

The Empress studied us. "You can always come visit then, both of you. Daniel and Elijah would love to have a cousin to play with."

Sure, so the twins could pull my red hair.

"Mysth's door always opens to you," the Empress added, sorrow filling her eyes. "I failed Tessa, as I failed many. If I'd known earlier, I'd have gone to find you and brought you both here to safety."

Then the Emperor was at her side. "You can't carry this grief forever, my love. People perished in the war, but those who sacrificed for a better world will be remembered. Every courtier of yours is living in your heart forever, and we have forever to remember them." He bent and kissed the glistening tears off her cheeks.

A love like that was worth dying for.

And now Ares and I had it as well. At the thought, I laced my fingers with Ares'. He was pleased at my gesture of affection.

"If Freyja had lived inside the Twilight Realm," a melodic voice rose from behind us, "her mate would never have found her."

A silver-haired beauty glided toward our table and took the empty seat. Her dark skin was flawless and shining. Mystic twin-runes sprawled up her temples.

The Empress inclined her head an inch to show her respect, as did Merlin.

But the Emperor scowled.

"And the First Witch would never fulfill her destiny to lead the future Earth," the woman said, fixing her eyes on me.

"Who are you?" I asked.

Ares shot to his feet. "Oracle! Here you are!"

"Here I am, and as you and your mate," said the Oracle as she lifted a glass of wine on the table and drained it.

"Hello, Consort Seth, still testy?" the Oracle said, her hair now coiling like white snakes. She hadn't forgotten that the Angel High Prince had bared his teeth at her. "I thought your beloved mate had mellowed you down after two decades on Earth." She then shook her head. "Why is it even a surprise to me that immortals never change?"

Fire of dark amber flashed in the Empress' eyes—a warning.

"I know, I know," the Oracle sighed. "You two are now a united front."

The Oracle turned to me as if wanting to defuse the tension. "My name is Nyx, which means one and many."

"I don't care if you're one or many," Ares grated. "You lied to me. You sent me on a fool's errand to amuse yourself."

"I never lie. I only skip a truth here and there," Nyx said. "Is finding and gaining your mate a fool's errand, Prince Darken?"

Ares sent me a glance and looked less pissed now.

"It all turned out perfectly, didn't it?" said the Oracle. "I didn't lead you on a wild goose chase. Your mate did, after I led you to her."

"If you just told me Freyja was the First Witch in the first place, I wouldn't have—"

"What fun can we have then?" Nyx said. "A little trial is healthy to a strong relationship."

"A little trial?" Ares asked. "I almost lost her."

Nyx gave a shrug. "But you didn't. Look how you hold her in your big, muscled arms. So possessive." Then she gave my uncle a knowing smirk. "Goddess Rhea also helped you attain her favorite daughter and never asked anything in return."

"She has my Forbidden Glory now," the Emperor grunted. He was only gentle with his mate. With others, he was still his old self—impatient and frightening.

Empress Rose gave them a wary look. "A little trial of fire can work wonders," she said in an offer of peace. "My beloved husband crossed the light years to find me after having suffered two thousand years of celibacy."

The Emperor gazed at his young wife, his eyes a bright silver.

Nyx looked at me with warmth, no longer carrying an air of irony.

The Oracle wanted me to live. If she hadn't sent Ares and he hadn't come, I would have let the curse of fire and ice decide my fate.

She'd given both Ares and me a choice by not revealing that I was the First Witch.

"Thank you," I told Nyx. I forever owed her a debt.

Ares sighed in resignation. "I should also thank you for leading me to my mate."

"What truly brought you here this time, Nyx?" the Emperor rose to his full and demanded, his wings tugging in tight. "It isn't only about my niece, is it?"

"I bear the final tide," Nyx scanned us all. "Soon, in less than a thousand years, magic will fade from the Twilight Realm."

The Empress' face paled. "Am I out of the favor with Earth Mother?"

"No," Nyx said. "But the time of change has come. Earth won't be like today. Magic will spread to the mortal lands, and technology will rise to full. Ares and Freyja's offspring will lead the future Earth, which will be plagued by wars, pollution, overpopulation, diseases, and dissension in everything and everywhere."

"That sounds really cheery," I said.

The Oracle ignored my sarcasm. Her sad eyes turned glassy white. She wasn't seeing. "Goddess Rhea's power will stretch thin. She'll also become the thing of the past, like the Fey. We'll no longer have an imprint on this planet when humankind completely dominates it."

"So we'll just fade off as the mortals' powers grow?"

Empress Rose asked as tears sparkled in her eyes.

"No, my love," her consort pulled her into his arms, his wings wrapping around her to comfort her, and she leaned against him for strength. "We'll go to a new home. We—all Fey and my Fallen Angels—will migrate to my planet Valhalla at the edge of the far galaxy. It isn't magical like the Twilight Realm, but it has violet seas, silver forests, and the most stunning night sky. We'll build a new future there. We'll adapt together."

He bent to give her a scorching kiss full of immeasurable love and passion.

The Oracle turned to me, and I wanted to shrink back. Ares supported me in his solid arms.

"Thank you, Nyx," I said. "But I don't want to know my future."

"The Fey will become myth in the mortal world," Nyx said, "as will you, the First Witch, and you, a Dragonian shifter, her consort, though your offspring will lead the nations and fight one another. Freyja, as an immortal, you'll be heartbroken and eventually fade when your mate is gone."

"Thank you very much for telling her that," Ares grated. "Will you just stop?"

I turned to Ares. "At least we have now and each other." He gave me a kiss that was no less scorching than the kiss the

Angel Emperor had bestowed upon his Empress.

"What about my curse?" I asked Nyx.

"What curse?" Nyx asked.

"Fire in my blood and ice in my veins," I said. "I thought you knew it all. Can Empress Rose heal me?"

"Your mate has healed you," Nyx said, "after he bit you."

My face flamed, and Ares grinned, happy to take the credit, and kissed his mark on my neck.

"And when you embraced your heritage," the Oracle added, "you reconciled the light and darkness in you."

"What about my death touch then?" I asked.

"Do you want it to remain lethal?" Nyx asked.

I pondered.

"I'm fine with the fact that you can touch only me, darling," Ares said. "There's no need for you to touch anyone else."

The Empress arched an eyebrow.

"The trait can pass onto our children," I said. "Do you want them to inherit it? You're immune to me, but might not be to them. They can be more lethal than I, and you won't have a chance to hold them in your arms."

Ares sighed. "Fine, let's get rid of it."

"You can now choose who gets to live or die with your touch, Freyja." The Oracle winked. "You're the First Witch."

CHAPTER 19

Atlantis Home

We flew toward the golden skyscraper where my new home would be.

Even from afar, I could see it was a great work of engineering—wild nature seamlessly immersed into the sophisticated, modern buildings.

Atlantis seemed to float in the air.

No wonder my father had seized this most advanced mortal city when he and his Reaper Angels had first landed on Earth.

We sailed over the marble bridge above the waterfalls. Ares' elite warriors lined each side of the wide bridge, raising their long swords to salute us.

The metal gate to the entrance of the palace gleamed in the sunlight, witnessing past, present, and future. One day, it wouldn't be there either.

My uncle had taught me how to summon my wings. They were a fabulous sight. As formidable as they looked, my flame wouldn't burn my mate.

Right now, I could fly beside Ventus, but Ares insisted on my staying with him. "A Dragonian never separates from his mate," he emphasized.

I would have a lot of free time to fly around when he was busy. He would get really busy.

Right now, Ventus was having the time of the century flirting with the she-dragon. She puffed a stream of fire, and he called, "Watch this, Belinda!" and sent his wind to chase her fire.

It was no longer "Freyja, look at this," or "Witchling, have you seen that?"

It was all about the she-dragon now.

"What do you think of Ares and Freyja's story, Belinda?" Ventus asked.

What story? Belinda asked.

"They ride into the sunset," Ventus said.

I don't see sunset, Belinda yawned. *It's morning.*

With a sigh, Ventus swooped toward the crystal roof, and the skylight unfolded beneath us. A hundred feet down there was a natural spring creek in a vast basin lit by artificial lights.

I leapt from Ventus' back, my flaming wings whooshing open as I dove. Ares also jumped. He dropped in a crouch and looked up at me with an adoring gaze as I slowly descended.

"It's a good show, right, Belinda?" Ventus turned to the dragon.

Belinda sent a gentle ring of orange fire toward the guardian of wind.

Ares pressed the device on his wrist armor, and the skylight slid shut in Ventus' face.

"Wait, Highness," Ventus shouted from above.

Ares ignored him.

Through the crystal skylight, I saw Ventus and the dragon flying away.

Merlin, who rode the dragon, would join Commander Darken. Ventus would tag along.

I'd managed to piece together some of the events on the way to Atlantis. Before Merlin had come to aid us battling Atlas' force, he'd been with Commander Darken. It turned out that the Commander had been poisoned by his pure-blood sons. Merlin had used his great healing magic to purge the poison.

The Commander had decided to let Ares ascend to the

throne earlier, so he could retire. I would persuade Ares to decline the offer. Who would want the burden of a kingdom? Besides, the Commander was still in his prime. He could kick around for a few more centuries.

I, as his heir's mate, would have to meet him soon.

I wondered how he would perceive me—an Angel princess.

But I wouldn't worry too much about it when Ares' gaze on me was hotter than the flame on my blue wings.

"What now?" I asked, my wings vanishing.

"Now we bathe," he said, "and then I'll take you to our bedroom to take a nap. We'll go see my father tonight. Tomorrow, there'll be a grand celebration in honor of my future queen."

I looked at him in horror. "I'm not ready. You moved too fast."

"Did I?" he asked as he gathered me into his arms.

"You said we'd decide everything together!"

"You're my mate, my wife, my future queen. That's a done deal. There's nothing left to decide on that."

"I mean the official thing!"

"You mean the party? You love parties, don't you, my darling Freyja?"

"I—"

His sensual lips slanted over mine, and his hand cupped my breast through the fabric. Every touch was a song of fire in my veins. My knees buckled beneath me. I could no longer think straight and argue with him when his tongue thrust into my mouth.

That probably was his purpose.

Not liking our clothes getting in the way, Ares tore them apart, until there was no barrier between us. He glided his hand toward my arching flesh and set me ablaze.

"You're mine now and forever," he whispered in my ears hoarsely, his erection a steel rod against my belly. "But this time, we'll go slow." He scooped me up and strode toward the water. "I don't care how fiercely you protest or beg for the wildest fuck. This time, we're going to make love."

While we made love under the sun and stars, he asked me, "Do you love me?"

"Yes," I said. And I didn't lie.

— The end —

Author's Notes

Dear Readers,

I'm glad you've come through to the end of Freyja's adventure. Next we'll go to the badland of the wickedest witch in the universe. You met her on *ThunderSong*'s bridge in *The Witch's Consort*, and you might also recognize the black-winged, tattooed Archangel Gabriel from *The Empress of Mysth*.

Gabriel falls through the crack of time and space into a savage planet while hunting down the Dark Lord of All Angels. Unfortunate for the arrogant warrior, the wickedest witch captures him and makes him her unwilling slave in bed and war. She isn't exactly nice, but she's very hot . . .

~ Meg

The Wicked Witch

I stood in front of a shuttlecraft that looked like a large, steel lizard.

The shuttle's rear had been squashed and the cabin door was half open. There was no sound inside. Its engine and power had been drained before it crashed, just like any other ships that had crashed on this planet.

As the silence prolonged, I believed whoever was inside was dead.

I waited for a few more seconds. With my ice magic shielding me, I stepped through the door.

Soon I was on the main deck. Just as I thought, the engine

and lights were dead, as was the lone species. Usually, I didn't give the dead a second glance as I went straight for the supplies. My witch tower's inventory was running low, and we hadn't had ships falling from the sky for three months.

Something caught my eyes.

The creature had massive, magnificent wings that were now limp. It was glossy, pure black. I couldn't resist striding toward them, and squatted to touch them. They were soft, sensual to the touch. They would be perfect decoration for the walls in my chamber, going well with my reputation as the wickedest witch.

I pondered on how to efficiently sever the wings and take them out of the jungle. Maybe I should come back after I took the food to my followers. Why would I care if they were happy with a full stomach? Simple. I needed them to keep fighting my war.

I shifted my gaze toward the specimen's face. His golden hair was still wet. Had he just stepped out of his shower before he plunged to his demise on this planet? He was big and muscled. A warrior breed with the rare combined traits of wildness and aristocratic refinement. A black-inked, mystic tattoo twined up from his corded neck to his temples. I could read the ancient symbols. But I would get to that later. It took time to decipher their intrigues.

The male wore a space uniform, which couldn't conceal his broad shoulders and hard chest. Too bad he was dead. I moved my finger and traced his cheek. It was still warm. Soon, he would be cold. Soon, his sun-kissed skin—which I favored—would go pale like mine.

My face was as pale as the bloodsuckers that occupied the other tower in the city. The lack of the sunlight in this damned place didn't help tan my skin. I had to paint red witch marks under the hollow of my eyes to make myself distinguishable from the vampires.

I wondered if there was enough sun from my original planet, but even if there was, it had left no mark on my almost transparent, pale skin.

The creature's eyelids fluttered. I jerked back my hand and jumped back. He stilled again. He was alive? How could one survive such a crash? I edged toward him cautiously and pressed two fingers on the column of his neck.

I felt a faint pulse, and at my touch, it grew stronger in an instant, as if it recognized my signature.

I blinked, and an electric current rushed into my arm through him.

I stood up, on guard.

The specimen groaned and opened his eyes. His foul mouth cursed.

I laid my boot on his neck.

The Angel

A blinding wave of pain shot through my wings, jolting me back to consciousness.

The damned vortex of time-portal had dragged my shuttle into it, and I had crashed on an uncharted planet with broken wings.

I needed to evaluate the situation, repair the damage, contact my crew, and get backup. But first, I needed to open my eyes.

I put a lot of effort into doing just that.

A female's perfume mixed with the most enticing pheromones wafted toward my nostrils. I had never smelled anything like that. It was fresh, bright, and enticing.

Someone was in the ship with me.

A booted foot stomped on my neck, its hard tip pressed against my jaw. A foot on a great Archangel!

Rage shot through me. Who dared stomp on me?

I flashed open my eyes to meet a brown leather boot wrapped around a bare, creamy leg. The boot was still planted firmly on the joint of my neck and shoulder, and the foolish offender had no intention of removing it soon.

I almost laughed at her daunting attitude.

My hand lashed out like a whip, grabbing the slender ankle. I could break it like snapping a twig.

A mortal female with a heart-shaped face stared down at me. Her raven black hair was pulled back in a braid, though a few strands drifted across her face. Her fine skin was pale and nearly transparent. She wasn't the type of beauty I used to bed, but there was something about her that made my heart pound harder than any female ever had, and I couldn't look away from her.

Perhaps it was because her large, piercing gray eyes regarded me as a cat studied a mouse. No one had ever looked at me as if I was their prey, but she took me as one. I narrowed my eyes. Soon, she was going to realize her mistake and would regret it to no end for insulting me in this manner.

The perfume I smelled earlier trickled off this female, yet I couldn't exactly figure out what species she was.

"Who the hell are you?" I asked roughly, giving her a chance to beg for forgiveness.

"Today is your lucky day, pretty boy," she purred, her voice sweet and silver, sending a strange chill down my spine. "You've just met the wickedest witch in the universe."

Pretty boy? I was ancient. I was immortal! I chuckled, half in amusement, half in annoyance.

That ticked her off.

An ice spear materialized from the mist, its sharp end pointing down, half an inch above my eyeball, the cold ice hissing.

I didn't flinch, but took time to rove my gaze on her. She wore only three pieces. Her leather shorts barely covered her shapely hips, leaving her long legs completely exposed. Her breastplates covered limited skin and didn't leave much to the imagination.

She hissed. The female intended to intimidate me, but I wasn't paying any attention to her spear. Rather, I stared at her glorious breasts. Evidently, she wasn't happy at me being distracted like that.

Then why the hell did she dress like that and flaunt her breasts in front of me?

I wouldn't mind telling her that she was far from my type. I was always drawn to blonde. This dark-haired female wasn't even among the most beautiful females I'd met across the broad universe in my long immortal existence.

Though there was something about this savage, but I wasn't interested in finding out. As my casual gaze moved down from her breasts to her flat, flawless belly with indifference, I felt a wicked punch to my groin.

My body grew heavy.

My cock hardened instantly.

I was aroused! At the same time, I was furious.

Wicked Witch (The Wickedest Witch Book 1)

Coming in November 2017

Also by Author

THE EMPRESS OF MYSTH SERIAL (COMPLETE)

THE EMPRESS OF MYSTH 1: ANGEL'S LUST

THE EMPRESS OF MYSTH 2: ANGEL'S OBSESSION

THE EMPRESS OF MYSTH 3: ANGEL'S INDECENT PROPOSAL

THE EMPRESS OF MYSTH 4: ANGEL'S GLORY

THE EMPRESS OF MYSTH 5: ANGEL'S FURY

THE EMPRESS OF MYSTH 6: ANGEL'S MATE

THE EMPRESS OF MYSTH 7: ANGEL'S WAR

THE EMPRESS OF MYSTH 8: ANGEL'S HOME

DARK CHEMISTRY SERIES

THE SIREN (DARK CHEMISTRY, #1)

"A flawless blend of sci-fi, YA fantasy, supernatural events, romance, adventure, action, suspense and intrigue ... The Siren is a one of a kind young adult story and the start of a truly captivating series. I cannot wait to read book 2 and see where this awesome adventure takes us."

THE PRINCE (DARK CHEMISTRY, # 2)

"If you are looking for a sci-fi adventure with cutting edge battles, sophisticated heroes and villains, lost ancient powers, and an impossible love interest that can only end in disaster, look no further."

<u>THE RED QUEEN</u> <u>(DARK CHEMISTRY, #3)</u>

"A powerful plot full of dire circumstances, intrigue, romance, mystery, and action, fans will certainly be captivated and engrossed."

<u>The Girl Next Door: A Small Town Romance</u>

"I would recommend Girl Next Door to readers who enjoy stories of first love, romance in general, YA fiction, and romance set in other cultures."

About the Author

Meg Xuemei X is an award-winning author of steamy paranormal and sci-fi romance. She finds it dreamingly delightful to be around drop-dead gorgeous alpha males who are forever tormented by her feisty heroines, formidable alien angels, wild shifters, haughty fey, dark vampires, and cunning witches.

She's visited the universe of *The Empress of Mysth*, *The First Witch*, and *Dark Chemistry*. Next she'll boldly go to the badland of *The Wickedest Witch*. At this moment, in her southern California abode, she's packing as many forbidden weapons as she can carry. Her favorite one was a magical whip.

Made in United States
Cleveland, OH
27 March 2025

15554742R00174